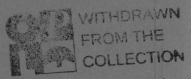

The Great
Far Away

ALSO BY JOAN FRANK:

Miss Kansas City

Boys Keep Being Born

The Great Far Away

Joan Frank

THE PERMANENT PRESS
Sag Harbor, New York 11963

Copyright © 2007 by Joan Frank.

Library of Congress Cataloging-in-Publication Data.

Frank, Joan, 1949—
    The great far away / Joan Frank.
        p. cm.
    ISBN 13: 978-1-57962-148-3
    ISBN 10: 1-57962-148-1
      1. Aging—Fiction. 2. Betrayal—Fiction. 3. California, Northern—Fiction.
I. Title.

PS3606.R38G74 2007
813'.6—dc22   2006051408

The Permanent Press
4170 Noyac Road
Sag Harbor, NY 11963

ACKNOWLEDGMENTS

Excerpt from the "Foreword," from THE SONG OF THE LARK by Willa Cather. Foreword copyright © 1988 by Houghton Mifflin Company. All rights reserved.

Heartfelt thanks, as always, to Ianthe Brautigan, Bob Duxbury, and the late, beloved Deborah Mansergh Gardiner. To Judith and Marty Shepard, for taking this book. And if I may— to the spirit of the late William Maxwell, whose work I hold close.

For my dear Bob, who loves this one best.

One must know the world . . .
        before one can know the parish.

                — Sarah Orne Jewett,
                        in a letter to Willa Cather

There was a period in my life when what was desired was very clear.

I remember it when I come upon a certain kind of countryside: what you might call postcard-land. Soft hills and dense stands of trees, lush and cool and patient, in which people have invisibly nested. Wind sifts and plays through the heavy curtains of green. Think, if you want, of the Pacific Northwest, perhaps of Vermont or the New Hampshire woods, or a Polynesian island along its jungly, windward side. (Think, too, of the backgrounds of certain medieval or Renaissance paintings: far hills, cypress trees, peaceful sky.) The light, battling through canopies of green, emerges unaccountably blue. A special blueness, this is. Dream-blue. The blue, you might say, of the horizon, the far distance where speculation is made.

The story I have to tell took place there.

Houses appear along the roads in odd rhythms as you pass, as if signaled by your passing to take shape only briefly, just the length of your gaze—houses in different states of age or dilapidation, so softened by weather and time that all color's given over to gray bone. No human is seen while you look, though artifacts of human life lay scattered: bicycles, potted plants, a weatherworn birdhouse nailed to a tree. Windchimes, panging faintly. A smashed tennis shoe. A bowl of clear water under the dripping spigot, moss lining its curved insides. All of it glimpsed in greenblue, ricocheting from all directions as if bouncing off a hundred secret mirrors. It drenches the vision, makes you sleepy. You look as you pass. No person, no movement, as if everything had been abandoned moments before. No sound but the slowed engine of your prowling car.

You pull over onto the road's grassy shoulder, and turn off the engine.

Bluegreen retreat. It was understood, thirty years ago, in the air around us. A pitted road. Houses more like cabins, patched together of used wood, out in the middle of grass pastures near the sea. The idea at first was to find enough money somehow, in that velvety, forsaken place—far from the metropolitan centers and their raucous striving. You scrabbled together some method of survival that spared you a fate far more dreaded than scrabbling: Straight Life. Straight Life meant drudging jobs, scratchy pantyhose, narrow shoes, razor shaves. It smelled of stale department-store shelves; pressed a thumb against your windpipe. But we young transplants to the grassy pastures were laughing at Straight Life then. Believing we had it fooled. Believing we could dwell safely away, if we burrowed deeply enough—dove into a good enough hiding place.

People my age may recall that time when they drive, even now, through the river town of Ferris—one hundred miles north of Sequoia (not its real name), where I now live. Gazing at the old houses under their gigantic trees and tall hedges, leafy protectorates in blue light, weather-ivoried paint curling off in chips, windows like blank eyes—a passerby may feel grabbed, pulled toward the quietude in a quick, senseless yearning. Yearning for what? To stop the dreary pattern, the ants' commerce, crawling back and forth with our crumbs of hoarding and trade. To hide away in blue retreat. To never be found. But now, after long years, we know better. At least I believe *I* know better. I remind myself—sternly—of what is not seen, over time, inside those dreamy, weather-softened houses.

A letter I received reminds me.

I am calling the river town Ferris, and I won't tell you its exact location. But I will tell you about some people I knew who made their homes there, who went about their days in rhythmic innocence, at least at the beginning. How did it start? Perhaps with the first young stakers, moving there from incomplete youths. Restless. Leaving college, worried families, silly jobs—because they were handsome, free, destined for special fates. They plopped down into the old northern California town like a team of parachutists onto a soft, flat field, determined to hunt for new beauty, and escape their former, pinching places. Some one or two of them had made their way by chance, or curiosity, to the little town. They'd told someone else who'd told someone else. They were boys then, really. Just boys.

They found jobs at first as waiters and busboys, as bartenders and landscape workers and flower harvesters. The 1970s were a sweet, open-ended time—at least, in Ferris they were. The boys loved the town's dusty main street and plaza, grocery and drugstore, its lunch counter smelling of malt. In the plaza's little square, grass and clover poked up between the bricks. Old-timers played chess under the drowsing willows,

or just sat and watched the sunlight change. The town was
having its gentle heyday, as did most such towns just then,
without knowing it. It was the era before a leisure class roved
the country in agitated herds, before health spas and cheese
boutiques and pre-wrinkled linen fashions, before restaurants with names like The General Store loomed up in what
had been empty grassy plots. Certainly it was well before
the resorts and bed-and-breakfasts, their lobbies selling heli-
copter tours, imprinted caps, save-the-rainforest candy. At
this blessed interval the sleepy town still thought the year
was somewhere around 1952. The young newcomers wandered around exulting. All the old advertising signs hung
untouched: the same stained barber pole, italicized script,
and movie-set storefronts snaggled together like discolored
teeth. The morning air was washed with jasmine and wisteria, pungent marigolds, and the brackish, damp, stone-
and-moss scent of the river that gave the valley its name: the
Rincon, never far in distance or mind, a body of water with
its own mind, whose tempers commanded the town's obedi-
ence during winter floods. (Every year those floods pushed
into the little stores and cabins near the water's edge, soaking
floors and goods and furniture with browngreen slime; the
weekly *Sentinel* always ran a front-page photograph of grim
storekeeps and welfare mothers digging out of the mess.
Every year the town council made serious talk about pre-
ventive measures, and every year it was all forgotten as soon
as spring warmed the air.) The air also smelled of brine—
stronger some days than others, depending on tides and
winds—since the bay where the Rincon emptied, a splay
of tributaries like a spread hand, was only ten miles to the

west. Water moved through and around the little town like a natural clock, and no one who lived there could not in some way always be aware of its soft ticking and swirring.

The boys, in time, drew the girls over. The girls came, like their brothers, escaping airless suburbs or universities, or jobs they had no patience for. Especially they came escaping parents, wrought about their children's ways. Parents, even the hippest of them, made demands. Stern, post-war rosters. Lists of obligations, spoken or unspoken. Oh, the obligations! Imploring, grieving, chiding. It fretted and wearied the growing-up children. They were impatient and curious. They were meant for better things, they knew. Everything was due and owing to *them*, not the other way around. They could not flee fast enough.

Randall Peter Winslow came to Ferris that way. Elated by the sleepy village, he quickly found a room to rent in one of those battered old Victorians tucked off in the hilly pastureland just west of town. He bought a rusting Ford Falcon (its windows wouldn't close) from his landlord, and persuaded the uneasy Mrs. Jinn, who ran the grocery in the plaza, to set him up a charge account, which Randy always made sure to pay up on time. He liked to keep his wetsuit in the car and take his board into the surf at Moreno Bay when the waves were right. Randy was a good-looking boy—most all who met him said it. His fluffy brown hair, eyes of light green, and compact, muscled body made people agree he might be taken for a movie actor, or at least a television star. That first year in Ferris Randy spent many hours, late afternoons, sitting on the Commons—the flat, grassy bank giving onto a wide, calm portion of the river, where concerts and picnics were held in summer. Hugging his knees, he watched the willows and eucalyptus, pocked with soft white light from the sun behind, droop toward the flowing surface, mingling their greens with the green of the moving water—a swirl of murk with silver and lime and chlorophyll. Randy

liked his job at the little senior community center, a flank of
ex-military barracks where he kept the old denizens amused
and fed; he was pleased to put into accountable order the bits
of money that trickled in. Soon enough he became the old
folks' advocate, ensuring they received their pensions or social
service checks, got their groceries and prescriptions delivered.
As he gained confidence he began to visit local businesses to
beef up funding for his operation's programs. Randy became
expert at grant-writing and lobbying as a matter of course.
And this knowledge would serve him especially well much
later. But all that is to come. In the early years he liked fun
as much as any of us—if we had any obligation at all then,
it was to make merry. He went to the cheerful bars favored
by the infiltrating young—former barbecue joints with long
years of meat smoke still in the air; rusted farm tools and
horse collars on the walls—the Corona Club kept an entire,
small World War II biplane suspended from its ceiling—and
where live bands that weren't yet famous gave their scruffy
audiences long, soulful concerts.

It was during one of these that Randy asked an enthusi-
astic young woman to dance.

Alma Collier was not conventionally beautiful, but had
a pleasant, pliant body, brass-colored curls, freckles, a brilliant grin. The two danced and smoked and drank with joy.
Alma proved to be as generous in nature as her coating of
freckles, her eyes nearly closing with merriment when she
grinned. As lovers Randy and Alma became one of the era's
founding couples, and slowly drew around them similar
friends who became similar couples: these wove themselves
into a basket of cheerful, grown-up kids in that weightless

era, steadily forming a new piece of the town's population. The young people were conscious of the visual impact they made, growing into their own easy beauty and vigor like shiny colts, lightness of youth carrying them.

New faces wove in by turns. Some few disappeared for natural reasons (nostalgia for a hometown, the rare death, the distant family summons). The jobs began at ladder's bottom and tendrilled up. Cocktail waitresses transformed into sales associates, receptionists into legal secretaries or chiropractors; a few jocks somehow struggled through to become doctors or lawyers; art dabblers became illustrators. The tourist trade, once idling, began regaining strength in the town—rumors of a desirable destination have a way of slipping out like telegraph code—and the young people began to notice the town's appeal to travelers: its verdant positioning near river and sea; patches of vineyards with small wineries on the property; fishing and camping. (The few real hotels in those days would only be found in Sequoia.) Several natural hot springs clustered near Ferris; one still managed a dilapidated campground and a cracked, mossy warm-springs pool. Down the road toward the sea stood a couple of barn-sized old restaurants, maintained by Italian families who'd lived there since their immigrant great-grandfathers sawed the first trees. Hewn of dark wood, with deep, cool, yeasty-smelling interiors and high beamed ceilings, those restaurants functioned like old Viking halls, echoing as oversized pitchers of wine and trays mounded with meats and soups and pastas passed hand to hand in the tipsy crowds. The young people looked at all this and began to understand—a few of them—that they could make what they saw into something large.

Something to pay off wonderfully well. Something with limitless potential for paying better and better.

The young bohemians, heeding the primal calls—*found a family, make a stand, make your way*—knew money would have to be drawn to Ferris so that they would not have to leave their idyll. A few began to experiment with ways to achieve the money. Marijuana and cocaine took their furtive turns, but these proved too unstable, too risky and costly—a couple of the young men even had to do prison time in Sequoia. As the young *arrivistes* cast about, though, something else was beginning to stir in them, though no one spoke it aloud. Some of the young people—especially certain of the men—began to want to triumph at their game. While never relinquishing the charms of country life, they began to want more than to merely subsist. They wanted to rule where they stood. Very slowly, the notion hardened into conviction: it was not enough simply to have money. It was necessary to live splendidly right there amid the raw green pastures and hills, with the morning smells of river and wisteria. The money for it could be mined, farmed, drawn to them there in Ferris—if they were imaginative. If they were resourceful. If they saw their chance, and moved upon it.

Randy Winslow was one of the first to grasp all this, and he moved quietly and steadily. So did Graham Payne, a local boy who'd gone off, after his mother's death, to university at the biggest-name campus in the county. Unable to keep his mind on studies, he'd returned in a tumble of confusion and dislike. Randy and Graham surfed together, drank beer together at the Corona Club when the bands played Friday nights, and tended a little shared garden of marijuana plants for their private enjoyment. They were of the same age, and of approximately equal measures good will, good humor, and good-times motivation. Casual spirit-brothers, hailing each other with honks as their cars passed on the two-lane; grasping a hand and pressing it heartily with the other when they came face to face in the drugstore or the surf. Music was jazz fusion, rock, rasta. Jug wine was cheap. The young people were cheerfully working whatever jobs they could find. They rented cottages, sometimes cabins or teepees by the river or out in the middle of the horse pastures, or they took apartments in faded buildings (painted ads for medicinal tinctures and animal feed were still legible on the umber brickwork along the streets). They threw potluck dinners. Clothing was from the Salvation Army outlet; the music was loud, the hair long, the grins uncomplicated.

What made the young people especially happy was this: each of them was becoming known and liked by the others as a necessary thing all his own, a player in an ensemble. Each felt beloved whatever he did or, more often, did not do. No background information was known; none was desired. This merry erasure of history pressed a warm poultice to all their young hearts, easing them out of the stiff, defensive postures held so long against sour parents—against Straight Life. And in this gentle air of amniotic Neverland, of unheeded pasts and screened-off futures, the young people played and worked and grew and put forth blooms, like the sturdy tea roses and morning glory that twined up fences and porch pillars all over Ferris.

Who were they? There was a lesbian scold, a dope-growing Adonis, a petite, spoiled sexpot princess, a melancholy gay

poet, a squinty-eyed homeless cartoonist with a ponytail, a
beautiful, lithe, and wise dancer, many excellent musicians,
a few divers (mainly for abalone), keen volleyball players,
and kayakers. There was a carpenter, a juggler, and a mystic
who actually dwelt in a cave above the beach at Moreno
Bay. There was a fledgling doctor, slender and blond, who
liked to push himself in daring physical feats: rock-climbing
and hang-gliding. There were puppylike younger brothers
with liquid eyes; bosomy earth mothers who dished up tofu
ice cream and smelled like allspice. The young transplants
delivered newspapers, made candles, started flower farms,
and sold honey. They opened, in time, little shops offering
smoothies, sandwiches, surfboards, bicycles, and imported
Balinese clothing. Saturdays they turned out for softball
games at the local diamond, a leveled field atop a green
hill fenced on three sides by eucalyptus trees; two brown
horses nosed the earth in the distance, cropping grass. The
sun might be melting along the horizon before a ballgame
was done, tarnished silver clouds trailing after it, glittering
yellow at their edges like the gilt edges of burning paper.
There was beer, weed, and much teasing and hooting as each
boy and girl poised over home plate, gripping the bat and
brandishing it high—and often the laughing young friends
would not be able to bear ending the day, and so would agree
in a flurry of shouts, as they packed themselves into dusty
secondhand cars, to haul off to one or another's house for
an evening meal. There the tape cassettes and portable ste-
reos would set to rolling, and people who'd brought rotisserie
chicken, potato salad, and chocolate cake placed the food on
the crowded table as they entered, and went in to dance and

eat and laugh. Eyes met eyes knowingly. A world had been invented somehow, precious and unique, and now, surely, it would always be theirs. Perhaps if they did not say too much aloud but only smiled, the spell that lightly netted them all, the brilliant cloak of enchantment, would hold.

Naturally, years passed. But for the young people, time seemed not to move. They would joke with each other for years about it, calling Ferris "the town that time forgot." And yet time, in quiet steadfastness, went ahead with what it had to. People earned money, took out loans, bought land, and built homes. They began to marry. In the drugstore, on Center Street, behind the flashing windshields along the two-lane roads, passing faces were still constant—if they bore a few new lines at the corners of their smiling eyes. Faces were still lit from within. It seemed in truth only days before the chunky babies were being toted along to softball games, or propped like fat dolls on reception counters for people to come running to admire—and mere days again, or so it seemed, before those babies became tall and muscled young people whose voices had dropped.

But let us go back now for a moment, to the time when the babies were not yet conceived.

Graham Payne had found Darla Messenger back during an interval of need.

His longtime girlfriend Annie (in those days, five years was a long time) had drifted to another man. Annie had consulted friends, thrown out the *I Ching*, and one day moved out from the little house she shared with Graham; for a brief while she stayed down the road in the apartment of Darla, her friend from work. So when Graham first knocked miserably at Darla's door it was to try to speak with Annie, to persuade her to return to him. But Annie was on another wavelength, as people liked to say then about separate ways of thinking. And for reasons he himself hardly understood at the time, Graham found himself at Darla's door one night after he knew quite well that Annie was no longer staying there. He was trying to avoid seeing Annie, or even hearing tell of her. But he was sore for company, and Darla, after some reflection, decided she was not unwilling to provide it. Soon they were almost always seen together around Ferris—the sight nearly comical: Graham so tall and bony, Darla well-curved and small. One evening the two drove out to Moreno Bay and spent the night on the sand before a fire they built, huddled close under a blanket, arms around each other. By the time they watched the sun rise they had decided to get married, and began to lay their great plans.

Darla Messenger came from a wealthy Massachusetts family which had begun, increasingly, to annoy her with its possessiveness. Her father was a contracts lawyer, and in the course of growing up she had probably absorbed something of his manner. Like many children accustomed to receiving the best, Darla already assumed that the best would continue to flow to her the way you assumed oxygenated air would flow into your lungs when you drew breath. She had come to Ferris to escape her parents' control and to commence an enterprise of her own, at which she never doubted she would flourish. Darla Messenger was pretty, in the ripe way all the young women of that circle were pretty then—sunburned, petite but strong, twinkling inside a certain energy field that might best be called *game*. Eyes danced in those years for little more reason than sheer gladness of the world to hand. It is a light that mostly dies out of the eyes of men and women after a predictable while. But we are speaking now of the time when that light touched itself off everywhere, effortlessly from face to face, sparklers begetting sparklers like a candlelight reel.

Darla's eyes were sharp and penetrating, as well as amused. Her family had taught her to assess a situation quickly, and to make it work for her. She stood in her apartment doorway that early autumn night under the bug-fuzzed porchlight, crickets still pulsing like sleighbells, and she took in the sight of Graham Payne. He was tall and brown, and had frizzy coppery hair and great sad dark eyes. His hands and feet were big. His lovely eyes so brimmed with longing it struck her as something fresh and unalloyed. She knew Graham had lost his mother in the recent past, that the family was respected, local—a line of ancestors dating from Sequoia's founding—and that they owned property there. A long local history counted for rather a lot then, as it still does in small towns and cities across the land. She did not send him away.

"What would you like to do?" Darla asked Graham that night, when it was clear he found himself unable to leave. The air held early traces of winter snap, a smoke and fir-tree smell, and sometimes an evening dove gave its alarmed, soft *scree* before flapping off suddenly, still trilling, to a better shelter. "Anything you'd like," Graham answered solemnly, watching her as if for instruction. The tall, sad boy seemed to be trembling on the porch like someone whose skin had just vanished, so that if he weren't bandaged up quick and tightly, head to toe like a mummy, he might collapse into a pile of pulpy tissue at her feet. "Let's have a walk," Darla said. She lifted her jean jacket off the hook and bade him come along. They walked slowly a long way, along the gravel drive and the dark connecting street, empty at that hour of people and cars. It was a moonless night. The gravel seemed to suck noisily at their feet, so that they felt a relieved light- ness to reach the sidewalk on Spring Street, which was so still they could have walked right down its middle had they wished. They talked quietly, sketching the profiles of their still simple pasts, staring down at the pavement and up at the stars. In those years the town gave off so little light that the stars crept close, very close and clear. The two young people looked up at the ageless configurations—Orion's Belt and one of the Dippers, and at some distance from these, the steady white eye of Venus—and they wondered at the unmapped darkness.

Graham and Darla found a big, airy farmhouse on the road up Patch Mountain, which was not really a mountain at all, but the biggest hill facing Ferris from the north. The farmhouse cost more rent than Graham wanted to pay, but Darla was firm. Her vision never faltered—the certainty that form commanded function, that you were how you looked, that valuation, therefore meaning, was whipped straight up out of appearances like a fluffy meringue. She did not say it to Graham at the time, but everything she would do and say, in all the years that followed, taught him. Mornings up Patch Mountain, in that particular time—it was some years still, remember, before the trucks came, roaring with uphill effort, spewing black exhaust, passing each other like giant burdened ants up and down that road to clear tracts for the townhouse estates—before then the hill was only scattered stands of trees, eucalyptus and oak and some fir, in pasture grass dotted with clover and a few mushrooms. Some of these were psilocybin, easy to recognize because they looked like little half-furled brown-gray umbrellas, which we would seek and eat—they tasted like earth—wandering around in the tender sunny grass laughing, the dew a scattering of fire-opal chips across the pastures. A scrubbed-pale sky met the hill's new green. In spring, ragged sprigs of wildflowers popped out: purple, red, and yellow. Mornings up there smelled like rain and baby skin.

Darla could look out her kitchen window and see deer stepping delicately between the trees, raising their mild heads to examine her, soft translucent ears flicking, and sometimes a fawn or two hopping after, white freckles over tawn.

The couple made a pleasant nest. Darla worked hard at her insurance sales (life, home, equity, and later, corporate). She proved good at it, and got promoted to represent the company in Sequoia. Graham told himself he was glad of all this, that it was progress expected in the adult way of things, the course people were supposed to take. But in a hollow, fist-shaped place behind his breastbone came a squeezing Graham could not explain and never spoke of. He was frightened, and did not want to go forward with the adult way of things. He wanted to live the way he had lived even before he had met Annie, during the days when his mother was alive and sending his allowance every week to the address of whatever room he was renting. You stumbled from bed whenever it suited you, drove to Jinn's and drank a quart of apple juice and ate a couple of Tiger's Milk candy bars, drove to the surf at Moreno and saw your friends, hung out smoking onshore if the waves were not good—perhaps you went on up to the eucalyptus field to find a softball game—and wandered back home after a few last beers at the Corona. Certainly Graham was terrified when Darla announced she was pregnant, but in the midst of the shortness of breath and squeezing behind his breastplate that always came with these attacks, he talked to himself very fast. He'd already grown so accustomed to a base level of fear that it seemed best to go ahead and get on with the story of life, right alongside his fright. Left to himself, Graham knew, nothing would ever be made to happen—and beneath that, being left to himself seemed the most frightening prospect of all. There was a particular sound that to Graham Payne was the most sorrowful reminder of his loneliness and fear, and that was the sound of a single dove, cooing its plaintive coo in the afternoon. If the sound came to him through the kitchen window from the fir-smelling hills, or from the stubby cypress trees near Stone Cove, he would stop whatever he was doing and listen, paralyzed, as if to something unspeakable.

Randy and Alma Winslow rented one of those decrepit little houses banged together at midcentury that still stood in the apple and plum orchards along the road toward the sea; these warping structures had likely once been farmhands' quarters when the fruit was grown in more ambitious quantity. (Many of the orchards were neglected and half-gone to wild after farmers decided they could profit better from vineyards—but in the years the young people were repopulating the town, a few set about to resurrect them.) Right away Randy started work to shore up the old shelter, and to add on a couple of rooms.

The two cleaned and hauled. They raided the Salvation Army outlet in Ferris for furniture and dishes, and Randy built them a bed frame. They went to the Sears in Sequoia for towels, sheets, and a four-inch block of foam for a mattress. They paid the old Portuguese neighbor who pastured horses a small fee for a load of manure; he kindly hauled it over in his Jeep trailer. They cleared a big plot of loamy soil, turned the horse manure into it, sweating, and planted vegetables. During the day Randy took the rattling dust-colored Falcon (it smelled of cat pee) to put in his hours at the senior center. Sometimes Alma would drive, dropping him there so she could have the car to do laundry and mail bills. They put plastic lawn chairs and cold beer out in front of the house to watch the evening come, with its sudden deep coolness and fog off the sea. And because they were some distance from the town the stars came wondrously close, peering at them in a kindly way.

The friends of our friends rejoiced in their joining, and in the way the days seemed to open out with such gracious, unplanned combinations. Annie had found her way to Bruce Mason, the schoolteacher she believed she was destined for. Bruce allowed himself to be persuaded by Annie; they were living together, and after some difficulty Graham Payne told himself he had made his way to a peaceable state about it, so that he and Bruce could even smile and talk at parties and ballgames. They liked each other well enough. The group of young people moved and breathed together in unconscious happy unison, like a great warm bellows.

That is when the babies began to come.

Ah, the babies.

They were fat and glowing and impish. Renaissance cherubs in tight curls or kinky wires or every-which-way feathers, flapping their arms and shrieking with pleasure. They were named noble, fanciful things, like Jedediah and Ariel and Skate. They had good food, fresh air, and sun; they regarded the observer with wet lips and eyes nearly filled by enormous irises of deeply pure colors. They laughed like fountains, patting the adults' faces with tiny chubby mitts, splashing in the sand where the Commons met the river. The young women who were their mothers kept them snugly-dressed and clean and sweet. The young women had been drawn, in a single mass swoon, deep into the yearning—craving suddenly, like creatures ill or wounded—to push a baby out from swollen wombs and care for it ever after. It made no sense when they inquired of themselves, but they'd kept after the project, frantic and unyielding. When their men were reluctant the young women fumed and pleaded, and the men, as is said, caved. Occasionally, it went the other direction: a few of the women had no wish for children, but at last gave way to their men, who were taken suddenly (and even to themselves, unaccountably) with hard longing for a small being to hold and form and guide, for heirs and apprentices, namesakes—the men promising on everything holy to share the work of it with their women. So out into the leafy sunlight marched those fat, glistening babies, one after another, black and brown and café crème and near-albino. They were named Heather and Prana, Cassidy and Rainbow, Jonah and Maximilian and Miguel. They played together in living rooms; they played at the river, their mothers attending in loose cotton dresses and wide floppy straw hats with flowers woven around the brim. They began arriving like plump door prizes to the potluck dinners, toted headlong under their parents' arms like musical instruments or stuffed sacks of rice, and the gatherings became livelier and noisier and a shade more complicated, but just as fun. When you thought about it, perhaps it was more fun than ever before.

Randy and Alma gave birth to blue-eyed Kira Louisa Winslow, born clenched up like an astronaut, with fine wisps of whitish silk on her head which shortly became brass-colored curls—friends later said she resembled the girl member of the twins on the soup can labels. Graham and Darla greeted (with relief, after some not-small tussling and a Caesarean section) Ethan Messenger Payne, fat as a sumo wrestler, with a thatch of black hair like a toupée, whose smiles pinched up the fat around his dark-lashed, deep brown eyes.

Darla used to stand the gigantic baby Ethan up on the table in Marlene's Café and, grasping both his fists, let his ham-thighs wobble along in pretend-steps, to the consternation of whomever might be eating lunch with her. She was fascinated by his whims and determined he should have

every freedom shy of mortal endangerment. Graham wondered whether other young fathers felt as irrelevant as he did
those first years. It astonished him to hold the hefty package
of flesh—to look into the puffy face so redolent of his, this
shocking being that he had somehow created. But when the
baby screamed or filled its diapers with foulness, Graham
could never completely fight off his horror and panic, and
in the chaotic flush of self-accusation to follow could never
escape the sense that he simply did not know enough, and
could never be sure enough of anything to be a real father. At
his center lodged a dread that someone in authority—some
secret society for catching out fraud—might find him and
drag him away. How could he feel so uncertain of everything, yet still be this little creature's progenitor? His pals in
the group of young friends, most of them by then producing
babies in intensifying surges like explosions of popping corn,
seemed to be making the adjustment well enough. There was
the usual joking among the men: rolling of eyes at lost sleep,
interrupted sex, exaggerated demands of women. But none
of the men spoke of stomach-twisting fright, of wanting
to run off or disappear. They seemed to be wearing their
new lives like a fresh layer of clothing—a down vest, say,
under which the same easy-grinning fellows they'd always
been stood warm and solid. How could Graham explain
to them how scrambled he felt, how scared? He hardly saw
the familiar countryside when he drove (thankful for the
excuse) to Jinn's for groceries. He knew less now than ever
before. In silence he carried the knowledge that he'd never
graduated—never made that mysterious leap to an adult's
easy confidence. More than ever he felt what he'd always felt
himself to be: a confused boy.

It was Darla who drove their days, who gave instant, strong resonance to their forward motion. If anyone had asked Graham years later how it had all come about, how the child had got reared, the loans obtained for homes and cars and trips, the schools found and paid for—he would have had no choice but to shrug and open his hands in genuine wonder: Darla. Her serenity, her strength, baffled him. All the assuming she did! On what could she base it? How could she always be so sure? Even if she were bluffing all the time—and he doubted she was—the effect was the same. Darla got what she wanted. In those beginning years she would sometimes place young Ethan in Graham's arms, and tell him she was going down to the office for a couple of hours. (Darla had resumed work as soon as the doctor said she might.) There were extra bottles of formula in the refrigerator, she reminded him, and clean diapers in the bathroom. Graham would stare numbly at her.

"You've got to bond with your son," she'd say to him. She did not say it unkindly, but looked intently into his eyes. By now she knew that Graham was afraid. She took it without fuss or comment, though it annoyed her. It annoyed her

more than anything else because of the time required to deal
with it.

"You'll be fine, sweetie. Office number's tacked up by
the kitchen phone, remember. Can you put some water in
the plants, please, and pull something out of the freezer for
tonight?"

She pecked his somber cheek, near his temple. Then she
kissed Ethan's fat one. With the heavy toddler against his
shoulder already wriggling to be set loose, Graham watched
her back the station wagon out of the long driveway and
guide it smoothly onto Patch Mountain Road.

Even the way she handled the car had determination.

Ethan began to wriggle harder and whine, so Graham
carefully set him down. At once the child, who wore only a
diaper and t-shirt, began his fleshy, stiff-legged scuttle across
the carpet toward the living-room window.

"*Mmmuh.*"

Ethan ran, Graham thought, like one of those lake loons
you see on nature documentaries, the kind that takes a long,
calamitous running start along the water's surface before it
can get airborne. Toes out, arms flapping. The baby arrived
at the window, slapped his puffy palms against the glass, and
stared forlornly toward where the car had taken its leave.

"Muh," he said, without hope. Graham's heart flattened a
beat. The toddler knew Graham was second-best.

Ferris was laid out like a zipper, with Center Street its main track down the middle, and fanning out crosswise from that—cushioned by wide, treebound yards and bushy lots not yet claimed—loose grids of shambling residential roads. Along these were scattered small, homely bungalows or low apartment complexes, some built in the WPA days. On the streets immediately off Center, a few homemade businesses—an arts and crafts store, its wares dusty, a hairdresser's called Heavenly Glamour. The copy center, travel agency, and music store would appear soon enough, like mushrooms after a rain. Then came the organic foods café and the boutique filled with handmade long skirts and round-toed slippers of wine-colored velvet. Not long thereafter, of course, would come the fitness center, the fancy restaurants, the industrial parks. But that part's ahead. The plaza square with its grocery and drugstore stood about midway down Center, and the town's oldest edifices tottered blindly to attention along either side, like very aged but dignified doormen: one an absurdly grand post office which had long ago—in a fit of optimism by the town's founders—been a bank, with Greek columns and elaborate cornices at their top edges. On the

corner of Center and Spring shone the oversized windows of
a car showroom. Inside, a single automobile sat on display.
A salesman wearing a suit seemed to swim around the car all
day like a lonely fish. The showroom's survival was a permanent mystery (no one ever bothered to question it, or even
talk about it), for almost no one in Ferris those days would
have dreamed of buying a new car (you made a trip to the
used lots in Sequoia). A coffeeshop faced the car showroom
from across the street, with red formica tables and sticky
vinyl chairs, where the old people, young mothers, and job-
less drifted during the day. Some of the town businessfolk
took their midday meal there, and sometimes Randy took
his funding prospects there to lunch.

    After Kira's birth Randy had got himself appointed, on
the local ballot initiative, to the position of executive director
of his center, and he began in earnest to scour for serious
money, as well as to find and invent every way he could to
root the work—and his own reputation—in the community. He hired an assistant, who doubled as the center's pub-
licist, and found better quarters in an abandoned elementary
school, where the doors were still bisected by slender vertical windows at the level of children's eyes. But soon Randy
would have to find permanent quarters, because the school
was to be reopened—so he was told by county officials
passing through town, whom he took to lunch. The population of Ferris, spurred and flushed with the new blood of the
migrant young who were now busy making babies of their
own, was climbing again.

    Randy and Alma were working hard in those years to
make good. *Make good.* Now there was a notion. Summed

things up in a fingersnap. Knead a hearty dough of your life, your family's little life: bake to perfection. Mmm, good. Dense and fragrant, warm and yeasty. Alma baked, all those years. Lovely things. Dinner rolls and bagels, scones, pizza crusts, and English muffins from scratch, for the adventure of it. She cleaned constantly, of course, and gardened, placing baby Kira, clad in only a diaper, on a blanket out on the grass when it was warm and sunny. Vitamin D in the sunshine, someone had told her. Alma kept the radio going while she worked and watched the baby, and sometimes she danced to the music by herself, or with the baby. Mild-tempered Kira was content to push her toys around on the blanket, studying their shapes and hefts, considering the sounds the plastic keys made when they clacked together, cooing, blinking at the melding greens and blues of the Winslow yard in the sun.

The soft silence of those mornings, interwoven with clean wind, seemed to Alma like a benediction. The air felt tender and cool. She often stopped her spading or sweeping to listen to the wind, to watch the hillgrass riffling around her and the crows making their crisscross flights. She would think suddenly about the way Randy leaned over to put a warm hand on her knee, or the way he relaxed back against his chair at the dinner table, lay his arm alongside the top of the back of her chair, and looked at her, his nose wrinkling with helpless laughter, when they both found something funny. *This is right,* she would think, without words. *And I am lucky, so lucky.*

Randy and Alma went to the tribe's softball games and potlucks, and at home they fixed stir-fry dinners with vegetables from the garden. Neither questioned the path which seemed to open smooth and clear before them, and when Kira arrived she only seemed the next sensible section along this preordained path, the baby's calm, pleased smile as inevitable as all the other roadsigns that seemed to pop up brightly at every turn:

On Track. Keep Going.

"A what? A campout?"

Alma must have murmured her startlement into the phone. It wasn't something the tribe usually undertook, though Lord knew they'd already done so much together as a tribe by now they may as well have been camping in one big auditorium for years. Like those Red Cross stations during disasters, where all the town's inhabitants sleep and eat in the school gym.

"That's right, doll. At Moreno. Everyone's showing up this time. You're not allowed to refuse. Bring a main dish, and water, and sleeping bags and swimsuits."

Mavis Hornby always called Alma *doll*, presumably because of Alma's disposition. It embarrassed and irritated Alma because it made her feel reduced to a child. *Unfair*, she always thought: she was a mother and wife and perfectly intelligent. Mavis was the lesbian scold. Lately she had dropped her last name, which she felt identified her with her former husband, who lived in Montana, and now she insisted people use her middle name, Regan, as her surname. So it was Mavis Regan this and Mavis Regan that. The sound at first rang stilted to Alma, like a brand, or a corporate name. The

Mavis Regan Charitable Trust. Mavis Regan Blueberry Pre-
serves. But after a while, as with any of the strangest arrange-
ments we can ever imagine, everyone just got used to it and
said it that way. Everyone liked Mavis Regan, though her
manner was always perplexingly sharp. Alma often wished
Mavis would stop trying so hard, so harshly, to remind them
all of alternative sexual orientations, a phrase just coming
into fashion at the time. If she'd only be a little kinder, Alma
thought. In truth, the youthful adult population of Ferris
those days was too busy and self-involved to be bothered
about militant sexual movements. Nobody cared whether
Mavis did it with German shepherds.

"So when is this thing again? Do the kids come too?"

"Absolutely the kids come too. Leeann'll be there."

"Ah." Alma conjured the image of Mavis's seven-year-
old, a skinny, angular girl whose disjointed, restless appearance disturbed Alma, and probably the whole group, as did
her behavior. The girl was noisy and confrontive, laughing
in a toneless, too loud, random way, pushing herself into
your face and staring open-mouthed (breathing phlegmily)
as if trying to figure out where you had hidden something
she wanted to steal. The child had red hair—a queasy, dark-
orange red, and the unfortunate genetic legacy of gapped buck
teeth. It didn't sit well with Alma to so dislike a child, and
privately she wondered whether Leeann's rowdiness wasn't in
part the result of her parents' early divorce, or maybe simply
Mavis's eccentricity. Then too, how could you ever separate
these things out? Alma had heard that Leeann gave her grade
school constant trouble, that Mavis was continually being
called in for conferences. But Mavis Regan was so prickly,

so hellbent on things being the way Mavis Regan said things were, that no one in the tribe dared bring up their discomfort with Leeann. Mavis was a republic of one.

"Just see you bring all the kid's favorite goodies."

"*The kid* is Kira, Mavis." Alma glanced protectively into the living room, at the pink package of flesh sitting cross-legged in her shorts, reading to her stuffed animals. Kira was five.

"Kira. Of course." Mavis corrected herself with theatrical exaggeration, as if to appease a lunatic's whim. "I knew that, doll. Kira. See you at Moreno at sunset, then. Friday night. And don't let Randy wiggle out of it. He works too much already. Volleyball. Marshmallows. Fun-o-rama. Right? Counting on you, okay, doll?"

Alma hung up, sighed, and thought, well, something different. Talking with Mavis always made her teeth tighten. Sometimes she fantasized making a brilliant retort that would, just once, shut the woman's mouth. But she always lost all words in the shapelessness of her anger. Anyway, what words could make Mavis change? Whatever words you spoke only invited more of Mavis's own: that flow of sharpness like a rain of tacks off her tongue. Forget it. Alma wondered what to fix, and decided on a big bowl—somewhere she still had that gigantic plastic bowl—of macaroni salad, with parmesan and red bell peppers and broccoli florets from the garden. Garlic and onion. Black olives. Randy might actually be glad to hear about the campout. He could use a break. Damn Mavis anyway. She shook her head, as if to shake off a whining insect, took quick steps to go and read with her daughter.

The year was 1983. And that is probably when the business I have to describe began.

When the cars commenced converging, lining up for the turn into the oleander-bordered asphalt, the June afternoon was turning windy and powdery. It was that moment of afternoon at the ocean when the sunlight lets go the reins; the light weakens and air cools just enough to make your skin lift and shiver. As people recognized each other's cars and began to extricate themselves—the children tumbling out in clumps of rumpled color, racing toward each other with heralding shouts while their mothers yelled crossly, unheard, for them to wait; the men easing out slowly, one arm already laden with packages or infants, waving to one another with wry, forbearing nods, wry at the state of themselves, their family-bound cumbersomeness—excitement mounted with familiar momentum. The young people flowed by habit toward these purposeless-but-for-love celebrations, and they carried deep affection for one another. Even the crabby and the shy moved along with the buoyancy that always swept them all up. Some giddy promise laced the air whenever the tribe came together. An expectancy. It was the beginning of summer, after all.

Family members carried duffels and backpacks, grocery bags and towels. They brought plastic bottles of juice and

water and half-gallons of milk and wine, big covered casse-
roles and thermos flasks and floppy inflatable swimming rafts
and tubes. A couple of people brought their dogs. The young
people and their gear and their children moved toward the
site (the first to arrive had picked it out) at the bottom of an
outcropping of rock ledge, topped by cypress. They moved
in ones and twos and threes, a ragtag caravan. The sand was
pleasantly warm, though it pulled at their feet more power-
fully with the loads they bore.

Alma let two of the men take the enormous tupperware
bowl (more a small tub, really) of macaroni salad, since it
was heavy and awkward. Gallantly, each with a hand to
either side as if the bowl were a child being lifted over the
sand, the men began walking crablike with bent knees, then
scampering, still bent-kneed, toward the campsite. The bowl
had no lid that would fit, so Alma had pasted several sheets
of cling-wrap over the top. The bowl was filled to the brim
with oily salad.

Alma had a clear premonition.

"Be careful!" she called to the men, hoarsely, several
times. As in a dream, the wind carried her voice away from
them, east toward the hills. She stood helpless. Her own
responses—her ability to act quickly or definitively—seemed
paralyzed, stuck in gel. The men had picked up speed and
were racing the bowl to the campsite. Why were they doing
this, racing the bowl? Alma went over it repeatedly in her
mind for weeks afterward. They were doing it because they
were still boys, impatient. Because it had occurred to each
of them at the same time, the way it does with boys, that it
would be fun to race. Because they may even have harbored a

secret wish, as boys do when they tease disaster, that disaster might take up their dare, step forward to meet them. And as though on cue, in one quick choreographed movement the two young men dropped the bowl.

It landed on its side. The plastic wrap fell away impotent as tissue, and the macaroni salad dumped headlong into the sand. Not all of it: perhaps the upper half of the bowl's contents streamed out. Sand and macaroni co-mingled brazenly. The macaroni looked like vomit or yellow-colored excreta from some huge animal, piled at a rude angle into the granular sand. The men stood laughing at the gross spectacle, glancing apologetically at Alma but unable to stop laughing, while the others walking around the scene at measured distance were laughing, too.

Alma stared, motionless. It had taken hours to prep and cook and put the giant mess together. Incoming members of the group, straggling forward on the sand toward the campsite and seeing the capsized bowl, at once began to laugh. Some of them hooted a witty comment or two. The men began trying to salvage what salad they could that hadn't touched the sand, scooping the bowl up through the spill awkwardly, hollering reassurances at Alma. There was still some left, they called to her. They were still laughing.

No laugh came to Alma. She stood staring. She bit her lip hard to make the sting stop at the corners of her eyes where tears ached to come. *Absurd*, to let this spoil the time. Absurd. Stop it. Stop it now. Randy appeared alongside her with Kira on his hip, putting a free hand to the back of her neck. He glanced into her face.

"Aw, that's tough, babe. But look, they saved some of it. Not freaked, are you? Gonna be okay?"

His voice carried the coaxing concern in marriages which is also a gentle injunction: *Be okay now, please.* Which in turn meant, *don't make me have to stop everything to nurse this.* He shaded his eyes against the afternoon, watching her.

"Yes," she said, turning toward the car to collect the next load to carry, so he would not see her ridiculous brink-of-tears.

Ridiculous. It wasn't so much losing the hours of work, she told herself. What was it, then? She tried to parse it out, her head ducking under the Falcon's trunk as she fussed with bags, grateful to be hidden by the trunk lid, breathing heated mustiness, motor oil, dust. It felt as though the others saw the salad as her main product. *Raison d'être.* Hail Alma, full of salad. She unclamped her front teeth from her lower lip, which stung from the steady pressure.

Alma took a breath, hoisted the bags. She lifted her knees, planting sandaled feet one after the other in the extravagant, dirty march through hot sand.

A figure called from behind.

"Doll!"

She turned to see the bony bodies of Mavis Regan and Leeann, slogging toward her through sand with their loads.

"Wait up! What happened to your salad?"

In summer, it stayed light until late. Children and adults gave themselves to a series of games and busynesses, wandering off to something different when they tired. The earth-mother women had spread blankets, organizing the food and the drink coolers. (Alma assisted.) A cooking fire was already sending up its nose-tickling, picnicky smell. Rex, the dope-growing Adonis, stood smiling in the onshore waves (they were small enough today, thankfully, for the older children) surrounded by a cluster of eager kids; he was offering bodysurfing lessons. Laurel, the lithe dancer who kept to herself, so mysteriously self-contained and beautiful the other women were a little afraid of her, jogged alone along the tideline in long, elegant sprints, legs lifting in weightless arcs. Mavis Regan and Leeann played sand-dodgeball in a circle with the younger kids—Kira was with them, concentrating ferociously as they all bellowed at each other. Leann's orange-red head could be seen from any distance, yelling loudest, dancing a jerky, gleeful puppet-dance. Big Dave, the carpenter who lived further out in the valley, stood in the sand by the volleyball net, shouting instructions to the scraggle of people assembling as teams on either side. Dave

made the impression of a Jesus-turned-lumberjack: a huge
fellow, beard, long hair, spectacles, a swashbuckling laugh.
His shouts from that distance sounded like salvos from a big
excited dog, and the real dogs raced back and forth among
the people, chasing one another and barking. Lane, the melancholy poet, sat watching, a loose aloha shirt hiding the soft
white middle he was shy to expose, an unopened volume of
Theodore Roethke at his side. Darla, pert and delectable in a
lime-green bikini, reclined on a towel, watching the athletes,
jumping up now and then to guide Ethan back nearer her
when his play took him too far toward the water. She would
squat with him at the edge of the wet sand from time to time,
examining shells and bits of gelatinous seaweed the color of
soda-bottle glass, watching him ponder the cold saltwater
rushing over his boxy feet.

Randy had already cast in with the volleyballers. So had
Bruce Mason, the lean, gentle schoolteacher, long admired
for his airpuff-soft set-ups. And so had Graham Payne.
Though Graham's feet were flat, his height made him useful
at the net.

If you'd stood back from this gathering, examining
it from some modest distance and elevation, say from the
highway that switchbacked along the hillside down to the
Moreno parking lot, and if there had not been so much
wind—you would have seen what looked like an ambitious
family picnic, and you would have heard the sounds that
people make at play on any beach in the world, sounds that
people with enough to eat and decent health and exuberant
hearts have been making for centuries. Play is mysterious—
or perhaps it is the one thing about us that is not. Bodies

raced and shouted, some of the youngest wailed, and the smell of campfire smoke and frying meat, of carbonated cola and beer, tantalized the nostrils. Along the coastline, like rhythmic punctuation, ocean waves opened and shut as if to declare *yes, it is so.*

When, after dark, the children were finally packed into sleeping bags inside two big tents, the dogs stationed by rope at their zipped-up doors (the women now glad for the dogs), around which the men had erected a fencing-in pen of wire-mesh (Rex's idea), the adults sat together in sweatshirts and baggy jeans and looked into the fire, holding plastic cups of chianti and cans of beer. The waves splashed quietly as if they too were sleeping, and in the darkness you could just see the flat lines of white foam extending and folding away.

Sebastian was the daredevil doctor. He sat like most of the others, knees up, long wrists loosely over them. Planks of his pale blond hair, like blunt paintbrush edges, stuck out from under the red St. Louis Cardinals baseball cap he always wore.

In the middle of the easy quietude he said, "Let's play the trust game."

What was the trust game?

"Where you fall backward and let people catch you," he said.

"It's good for nervous Nellies," he added, as if prescribing a medicine.

Sebastian was known to have enlisted with every Outward Bound trip you could think of. He'd spelunked, scuba-dived, been towed by a motorboat, and lifted far up in the air, strapped into a human-sized kite. Sebastian was thin,

pale, handsome in an ethereal, Pied Piper way. As far as the
tribe knew, he had no girlfriend. Perhaps he was getting over
a breakup with someone, from wherever he lived before.
(He had a barely-discernible accent.) Or perhaps no young
woman was eager to keep up with him. Cheerful, brisk, excit-
edly preparing for his next adventure, Sebastian was someone
you were always glad to see. The young people liked him
the way they liked everybody in the tribe. They never felt
queer or overawed that he was already a doctor—possibly
because their bristling good health was an unthinking given
for them, give or take the yearly colds and flus. The most the
tribe people ever did was ask him occasional shy questions,
and he graciously gave them advice for free.

Sebastian's eyes were of such a weak, thin blue they seemed
almost the color of water. He could be a prince from a far-
off kingdom, thought Alma, as she watched him unfold his
long, delicate body to a stand. A prince of snow. She thought
of green ice and dark gray skies; Nordic islands, landscapes
from a television program. In fact Sebastian was of German
origin, but she would learn that much later.

"Who wants to?" He looked around.

A few people murmured. A couple of the men got heavily
to their feet. Dave the giant carpenter was one of them, and
everyone laughed.

"Who's gonna risk catching *him*?" people teased.

Sebastian wasn't fazed. "I will," he smiled. Big Dave,
exonerated, lifted his chin at the scoffers.

Sebastian kept up his rally.

"Come on, guys. It's fun. It's good for you. How much
other stuff can we really say that about?"

"Sex!" shouted some of the others, in unison without having meant to be. Rich laughter. Soon Sebastian had a number of the young men and women staggering up. He paired them off arbitrarily as he walked around the ring in front of them, pointing an index finger toward each partici-pant like a camp instructor—you with you, you with you—each individual in the pairs to take a turn at catching, a turn at falling. Those who still sat on the sand moved awkwardly out of the way, scooting their butts like chimps while they balanced the drinks they were holding for the others.

The fire made the only light.

Lane the poet got paired with Rex. Mavis Regan stood with a skeptical hip cocked. She had been partnered with Laurel, who waited wordless and peaceful, a musing priestess in her terry cowl.

Mavis raised a hand. "Do we get to sue if we're injured?"

Randy had been assigned to Darla. Darla had urged Graham to get up and try it, but he shunned the idea and quickly scuttled out of range. Graham liked Sebastian, but disliked looking silly. He slipped to the back of the big doughnut-shaped ring of young people—perhaps there were thirty of them there that night—and away from the fire-light, lit up a joint, and strolled off down the beach with a couple of Big Dave's carpentry assistants. Alma found her-self paired with Bram Parnell, the ponytailed cartoonist. She worried that he might not have bathed too recently. Bram wasn't known for regular bathing, though he was a dear and talented boy. Alma admired his sketches and cartoons in the Ferris *Sentinel*, and liked discovering the new ones, tacked boldly over the ads for housecleaning or babysitting

on the bulletin board outside Jinn's grocery. (She always
wondered who finally took the cartoons down: probably
Mrs. Jinn.) The drawings parodied well-known politicians,
but sometimes they were funny caricatures of local person-
alities, merchants, or customers he sketched during the day
in Marlene's.

Sebastian clapped his hands for attention. It appeared he
did fully intend to catch Big Dave.

He must know martial arts, thought Alma.

"Okay, everybody!"

Sebastian called out procedure.

"Catchers, position yourselves. Test your angles," he
yelled. "Make sure there's no chance you're not squarely in
line with your faller for a clean catch."

Faller, thought Alma with amusement. Occupation? Faller.

"Fallers! When I count three, take a big breath and exhale
as you go back. Fall straight back. Arms out of the way,
remember, body loose. Envision your partner behind you,
like a stretchy steel net."

"Ready, everybody? One, two—three!"

Down went the dark vertical shapes of bodies, amid
shrieks and exclamations of *Wow, man! Cool!*—and afterward *Upsa-daisy!* and *My God!*, amid outbursts of laughter.
You couldn't see much in the firelight. Nobody was hurt.
Sebastian caught Big Dave handily, to Dave's delight. There
followed a babble of excited commentary, both mocking
and sincere, about how it felt to overcome the primal fear
of falling. Alma had felt Bram's arms hard and determined
immediately under her, breaking what really had been a
frightening stab of physical fear. Strong boy, for a cartoonist.
She felt fonder than ever of the skinny lad, turning to him in

a whoosh of relief.

"Thanks, Bram." She gave his shoulder a comradely squeeze. "Well done."

Bram squinted and gazed at the ground, for all the world as if he might tip his hat, climb onto a horse, and gallop off.

"You're welcome."

Alma knew he was flattered. He didn't smell too bad, really. They all smelled of campfire smoke now anyway.

Darla had no qualm about falling onto Randy. They were nearly the same height—they'd both been teased about it, because most men were much taller than Randy, and Darla, compared with many women, was considered a shrimp. Fact was, Randy was actually a full head taller than Darla. And he had the build of a human piston. He could probably have lifted a car. He stood ready behind her, relaxed, grinning his moviestar grin. On three she threw her arms out and sailed herself backward. Randy caught her lightly, easily, with a little bounce.

"Hup! There we go!"

And that was when what happened, happened.

Now: it may strike you as strange or improbable, and you might reasonably wonder how it could have come about this way. But the truth was, it did. Maybe because the two had never in their lives given any thought to such a thing.

Shock, was how it felt. In the instant she was against him, it was shock.

A long, preposterous beat followed. A stretched-out moment of the two staying exactly there like that: him stooped over her head in a half-squat, arms warm and strong under and around her. Her arms, also warm, molded over his—the way they might have over the armrests of a chair, or grasped the ropes of a swing. Holding. Holding. Neither spoke. Neither moved. Pandemonium rained around them. In the firelight Sebastian and Dave stood noisily congratulating the others. People were retrieving their drinks, gabbling. The dogs, straining at their sentry posts by the children's tents, jealous of the merriment, woofed softly.

Shock, was how it felt.

After many silent, stupefied beats, Randy Winslow sank down until he was sitting on the still-warm sand in the darkness, like a man upon whose head someone has broken a heavy bottle. He was still holding Darla Payne around her ribs, under her breasts, from behind, as if he'd just dragged her from water. She shifted her bottom so that she sat tight against him, her back flush against his chest, and his arms made the adjustment. Her own hands and forearms still held warmly to his forearms. With no comprehension, Randy simply lowered his chin alongside her head until it rested against the tender curve where neck met shoulder, among brown curls. Slowly, in bewildered reflex, he closed his eyes and carefully, deliberately pressed his mouth there, to that place. He breathed in deeply—as deeply as he had power to.

Shampoo, perfume, firesmoke, seasalt. Cocoa.

Her head rolled slightly, and she was awash with goosebumps. Then the tension of vigil returned, and she kept very still. Her arms still covering his.

He smelled like burnt angel food cake and bourbon.

Neither spoke a word.

Around them the silhouettes of whooping young people in the firelight raised and lowered like shadows of carousel horses: tropes on a turning lamp. Reaching and turning, whirl of chatter and motion, here and there flecked in gold. Their voices melted to a looping roar, motion thickened and dulled, a wavy smear.

A backdrop.

It's time to allow a number of years to pass.

These were the years in which the ambitions of the young people began to clarify in serious ways, and the town of Ferris began to change. The young adults had acquired small children and property, or they were en route to acquiring those things. They were gearing up. It was the time when careers began to take purposeful strides, and blueprints were drawn up. A new shopping mall was being built at the north end of Center Street, though some of the oldest citizens of Ferris mailed protest letters—a few got up petitions—and the little *Sentinel* blurted its alarm. In this mall would be a multiplex theatre, the town's first, a big supermarket, a national drug and pharmacy franchise—which everyone knew would not be good for poor Mrs. Jinn, nor for the Merit Drugstore in the plaza square, still operating its tiny lunch counter. The new mall would have a frozen yogurt café, and also something no one had yet conceived of: a real estate office. All the town's property transactions, since anyone could remember, had been handled in Sequoia.

Despite the steady infiltration of events like these, which most would later agree were only sensible, necessary

improvements—perhaps the most remarkable feature about
Ferris (when you thought about it) was its stubborn and
unashamed walling-out, in the willful minds of its population, of the workings of the world. The interim years we
speak of were full of critical markers in history, as most
anyone now can attest. But Ferris people—there's no other
way to say it—plain didn't want to know. If it didn't have
immediately to do with them, it wasn't happening. And the
curious thing was, while you were in the midst of living that
way—of ignoring the world, I mean—it worked fine. No
one paid attention to the news, except to cluck in a glazed
way at the headlines from the *Metropolitan Express* out of
Sequoia, if you chanced to look at the well-thumbed copy
someone always left on a table in Marlene's, bought from the
rust-veined machine outside. Nighttime television news was
one more soap opera. People followed their favorite radio
music, of course, and went off to the *Star Wars* movies. But
the news from the world always seemed very far, very bad,
hopelessly unresolvable. So Ferris people blew it off, as we'd
say. In those days nobody made you feel bad for it. You slept
better, digested your food better. It was simpler to turn your
thoughts to what was at hand. And there were so many such
matters to tend to.

Graham Payne, for example, needed to get a job.

He had no heart for any more school. The couple of part-
nerships he'd tried with friends (the surf shop, the vitamin
supplements) never returned enough to be worth the time.
And his mother's allowance had stopped with her death,
of course—a moderate lump sum was to be made out to
him, perhaps in a year or two, when her estate was settled.

Graham's father was long dead, an early heart attack during his work as a railroad switchman. (Sequoia had once been a prime rail hub, a loading center for shipping fruit and produce south.) Graham's mother's house and land holdings had been willed to her younger brother Winston, who lived on the island of Guam. On Winston's death his holdings would revert equally to Graham and to Winston's nephew and niece in Allentown, Pennsylvania. Graham had received an explanatory letter from the family attorney in Sequoia. His mother, knowing Graham's nature, had hoped to urge him to be more assertive in finding a vocation after her death. Her immediate bequest would amount to a small bonus. (They could start a college fund for Ethan on it, Darla had been quick to suggest.) The Paynes had been living on a cash gift from Darla's family, offered as a wedding present (though they'd never thought much of Graham; they made that clear), and then on Darla's income, when she went back to work. Graham could no longer coast, as we called it. Graham hated and dreaded the world of work, and in his heart knew he was everything the world of work hated. He despised straight clothes and unctuous courtesies, and all the rest of the phony toadying bullshit of clerical ladderclimbing. He'd checked around. He'd seen the airless county offices, their fluorescent lights, the workers moving about inside like B-movie zombies. Straight Life buckled him with revulsion, as it did many others in the tribe. The only reason Darla loved her insurance work, she claimed, was her autonomy: she kept independent hours and traveled on an expense account.

In fact, Darla seemed happier than ever. She seemed to float and flutter through the house getting ready for work,

intensely affectionate with Ethan—singing and waltzing him
around the room for dizzying minutes, to his baffled pleasure; he'd laugh and reach up when she set him down. "More,
Mama!" And then she always had to leave, and Graham was
left to face Ethan's wails of loss and get him ready for school
in the bargain. Darla's eyes shone; she seemed prettier. She
was gay and thoughtful with Graham, but her attentions felt
antic, revved up. (These were not perceptions a man articu-
lated in conscious words. They drifted in atmospherically,
like passing wisps of a puzzling, fruity scent.)

It was at about this time, on a Monday morning after
Graham had dropped Ethan at school (held now in the reac-
tivated buildings) that he found himself pulling into the
unpaved lot beside Marlene's in town. He had an idea he
might have a look at the help-wanted ads. It was September,
Indian summer. The morning fresh and fair, intense warmth
already seeped through, hinting at the cruel heat to come.
Trees and grass and vineyards still vibrated in high summer
green. The sidewalk had been hosed off for coolness, gave
up a sweet, relieved breath of wet stones. Graham pushed
through the belled screen door and it made its announce-
ment, the *ching* of an old cash register.

"Well, if it isn't Graham Payne."

Across the near-empty room Mavis Regan looked up, put
down her newspaper, and eyed him.

"What brings you out into civilian life, honey?"

She was sitting by the window. A half-full coffee and sec-
tions of the *Express* littered the table.

Graham sighed. Mavis was hard on people. Her voice
had a way of hurting your ears, with its built-in sarcasm—a

bit like the voice of the wicked witch in the Oz movie. A kind of scornful squawk. Graham had no energy for thrust and parry.

"I need to get a job, Mavis," he said as he walked up.

"Of course you do, dearie. It's all the rage. How come? Weed prices not up to snuff?" She pushed newspapers out of the way and slid a chair back for him.

Graham felt his chest quicken with anger; he checked himself. Graham had something that surprised and touched people for its sheer archaic simplicity: good manners. (His mother's training, and his own kind instincts.) He sensed that Mavis Regan's shrew act was some sort of shield, but he hadn't the will to figure it out. There was a phrase he'd heard, about throwing good money after bad. Energy, same thing.

"Mavis, I don't deal anymore. Since we had Ethan. You know that."

"Right, Graham-the-man. Delighted to hear it. What's your pleasure? Want the classifieds?"

"Sure, Mavis. Thank you. Thanks."

Graham sat down. He wished like hell that no one he'd known had been in the café this morning, but in the Ferris of that period, such a circumstance was almost guaranteed to be impossible.

"Coffee please, Marlene," he said to the woman who stood at the table with a stained chef's apron over her slacks. She wore the numbed forbearance of all the diner personnel we've ever known or seen or—many of us—been. Patient, laconic, tired.

The place held consoling smells of toast and bacon, overcooked coffee.

"How are you lately, Graham?" Mavis peered at him.

He shrugged. "Alright. Job hunt's the big humbug right now."

He wished, urgently, to avoid a chat. Leeann, now 11, was a pain in the ass, and Mavis was a divorced, *nouveau*-militant lesbian mother with a part-time job at the pharmacy in the plaza square drugstore. That was quite enough to know. He rattled the employment section open, shook it smooth, folded it back on itself, folded it twice more. He propped the resulting portion against his saucer, and leaned toward it.

"Graham, have you considered the new mall?" Mavis put her chin in her hand.

He looked up, trying to keep his face polite. She couldn't *not* chat.

"Not really. Why?"

"*Real estate* office," Mavis Regan said. She modulated the words the way a fortuneteller might say *handsome stranger*.

Graham began to wish he'd simply bought a paper and taken it home.

"What's that to me?"

"Think about it, honeybunny," Mavis said. She spoke with a crafty light in her eyes, another of Mavis's signature behaviors. Her eyes often seemed to bulge with this smug significance, as if she were guarding a magic secret. Graham reminded himself that the bulging-eyed business was part of her act, but it always troubled him because he himself was certain of nothing.

"You think I should be thinking about real estate work?" He poured his cream and took a tentative slurp. Sunlight, not yet high enough to angle directly into the window, covered the leaves outside with a yellow-white glare.

"You'd be independent," Mavis said. "No kissing up to straight bosses. You could maybe cut yourself a good deal down the road. And if you got a job at the mall office you wouldn't have to commute anywhere."

Graham looked at her. At first the notion seemed alien, but as he sat there (the muffled clinking of dishware and pans in the kitchen) it began to tease at him.

"Mavis, what made you think this up? What gave you the idea in the first place?"

Her brows hiked. She glanced around the empty café, leaned forward.

"I'm about to defect to the mall, myself," she said in a low tone.

Mavis couldn't say anything without drama, Graham thought.

"What do you mean? You're quitting the Merit pharmacy?"

"Yep. Getting a better-paid gig with the new Rite Aid coming in." She pressed the napkin to her mouth, crushed it, dropped it by the coffee saucer. She fished some coins from her bag, tucked them under the saucer.

"Best you not say anything about it for awhile though, thank you very much."

"Why not?"

"Because I *haven't done it yet!*"

She grinned, eyes flashing.

"But I will, honey. You just watch me."

She rose, shouldered her canvas bag. Mavis was skinny and bony with almost no shoulders—Graham wondered why the bag didn't slide off—and wore her light brown hair in a stump of a ponytail, the short hairs falling out around her face.

"Gotta go, Grahamie baby. Going to the *current* job, then collect my kid." She grinned again, her quick, facetious, punctuating grin.

Then with no segue, Mavis Regan's demeanor changed. She put a hand on his shoulder and looked at him fixedly.

"Graham, take care of yourself, okay?" —her voice earnest, for a change.

He couldn't make her out.

"Yeah, sure, Mavis. You too."

More drama, he guessed. Who knew. All Mavis needed was a cigar and Groucho glasses.

She stood considering him a moment, head to one side. Then she patted his shoulder and strode out, and the screen door *ka-chinged* its old bell.

On a sunny Friday morning one year later, Randy Winslow stood at his back door with a mug of hot coffee, looking due east to the cleared site on his acreage. The flatland made a seam with the mild rise that began there. He let the brilliant bluegreen of pastures and hills flood his vision, felt the pleasant ache of his pupils contracting in the influx of light. He had more dominion, more to answer for now, than he might once have dreamed. The load of it made him quieter, his gaze more inward, his mouth tight. He was building a new house on the land, land now their own. That is, the bank was now their landlord. He and Alma had taken out a loan and bought the property, finally persuading old Mr. Pacheco, who'd rented them the acres (and brought them horse manure when they were setting up), that he and Alma would make Pacheco's adjacent plot the more valuable by improving their own.

"How does it feel, owning all this?" a friend had marveled to Randy, gesturing wide at the pastoral acreage.

"It feels like debt," Randy answered without smiling.

He and Alma had found a Waldorf school for Kira, and to help with the costs of things Alma had taken a half-time job with the county, testing workers' hearing. She went around once a month to the different departments of their big, penitentiary-style building in Sequoia and outlying areas, in a little van like an ice cream vendor's, with a soundproof booth. One by one the workers came out of the building, blinking in the sun, glad for a sanctioned break. Sometimes they snuck a smoke—reeking of it, to Alma—then stepped up inside the little booth and put on heavy black bakelite earphones. With Alma seated at a writing stand, watching through a window, they held up a finger each time they heard a faraway tone pitched high or low. Alma would mark her charts, send them off to the evaluating company in St. Louis, Missouri; later she'd collect and mail the results. She said she liked the work. It let her meet folks.

That pleased Randy, because it helped that Alma should be pleasantly preoccupied while he was conducting a love affair with Darla Messenger Payne.

Now what is there, truly, to be said about this? What can you say about carrying on an affair outside of marriage in a small town that will not sound bitterly stupid? Randy couldn't have answered with a clear and reasoned reply. And if dumbfoundedness may be usual for others in his predicament, it was not usual for Randy. Because everything Randall Peter Winslow had undertaken, in all the life he'd lived so far, had been clear and reasoned. Starting with finding Ferris in the first place: simply the ground-floor impulse for a healthy young man. *Seeking my fortune.* A passage so fundamental, so common and ancient, it proved the clock of life was running correctly, and the world, noting this with relief, took off its hat and bowed low.

He sat down on the warmed back step, coffee mug balanced on a knee, and shaded his eyes. Scents of the river and the sea veined the morning air.

Randy was on schedule with the spoils of fortune-seeking. He directed a large operation, well-funded by federal and state budgets (through ballot initiatives, and Randy's tireless lobbying and grant-writing skills). The county had authorized the building of a new senior center in Ferris, on River Run near the Commons. Randy kept whatever hours he wished. He had a private office with a view of the willows and eucalyptus that canopied the river (though you couldn't see the river itself), an administrative staff, and the gratitude of a citizenry on behalf of its aging parents and grandparents. There was talk even then that Randy should run for a congressional seat representing the Rincon River Valley district. It made perfect sense to anyone who thought about it. People had always liked Randy, straight from his arrival in Ferris, and this, too, was unusual, because small-towners don't often take easily to strangers. They'd liked Randy for his buttoned-down sincerity, his can-do-ism, his energy and good sense. They were pleased to see that their trust had been founded.

Now he was enmeshed in the viral growth of subterfuge and lies that a love affair commands.

He'd never asked for it.

He'd known her from parties. Their kids had been born around the same time; of course he and Graham had been buds from young-guy days. Here he felt a terrible cramp at his center: Graham. The two men hardly saw each other anymore as their schedules heated up; when they did their greetings were brief, distracted. Randy's eyes narrowed a moment to see—oh, the mind is infinitely resourceful—a little holographic replay of the two of them bobbing on their boards in black wetsuits off Stone Cove, awaiting the next shapely set. Once a small school of about a half-dozen porpoises had suddenly arced and dived right between the two bobbing men, blithe and shining, one after the other, blueblack angels. He and Graham could have touched them. He saw himself and Graham lifting icy beers in the smoke and noise and music of the Corona. My God, how little weight they'd carried!

But the night of the silly game at the beach, there had come that electrocution that neither he nor Darla were in the least prepared for. Out of fucking nowhere. That—meltdown. Holding her unexpectedly against him. Every fiber of him awakened, blazed, shock and confusion.

Everywhere she was next to him, seared him.

Her fragrance, something fruity in it. Her delicacy, her curves. Some mystery she kept about her actual person, even though she'd been as naked to him as the day she was born, naked and opened, daring him, and they'd had every manner of sweating sex they could think of. Yet he'd feel her withholding something—he couldn't say what, or why. A gesture, a reticence. It drove him crazier for her. Crazy to get at the withheld thing. To wrap her, infiltrate her. *Solve* her.

Her mischievousness. Oh, he'd come to know it.

It was a new life, as if roused from a long, druggy hibernation. He'd had a few girlfriends before Alma, but never— he searched for the word—this *charge*. He wondered, with a flush of pride, whether it was happening because he was older. Maybe you could apprehend things at 35 you didn't have the gear for earlier. He felt like a bionic man, brimming with strength and agility and alertness. His eyes seemed more finely attuned to light, the colors extra-saturated. Food tasted blissful. It was like owning a secret Christmas, going to sleep at night, waking in a kind of breathlessness. His heart pounded to think what had already happened, to think what might happen the next time he could see her. If he let these musings continue, however, he would begin to get hard and have to switch thoughts fast, especially if he were at home.

Home.

Its fullness, and warm scent of dailiness.

Randy examined the ground beside him. He registered, without consciousness, Alma's pots of geraniums, petunias, and marigolds. Their spilling colors—scarlets, purples, rubies, and butters—clay pots bordering the porch steps. He set down the coffee, picked up a rough stone, and flung it with a clean whipflick of his wrist. It sailed in a wide unwavering arc, landing just where the taut string line, tied from post to post, marked off the dimensions of the new house.

Kira. A beauty. Those brass curls. And smart. Her drawings for him covered the refrigerator, and at his work desk, alongside her teak-framed photograph, he kept a lumpy cracked bluegray ceramic bowl she'd glazed at school for him when she was younger, the wobbling letters *Daddy* painted in black around its edge. He and Alma had looked at each other and laughed at this homely solemnity; Kira's face had crumpled until he quickly explained they had laughed because they were delighted, that the bowl was beautiful, and that he *especially* loved it.

In fact, he and Alma had laughed not so much at the homeliness of the gift as at the comic irony it pointed up: a couple of hippies-turned-bourgeois, now well into reaping recognizable fruits of the bourgeoisie. He used to try, as a deliberate torture, to ask himself how she'd see him—his Kira—if she knew.

But the mental screen went blank on him each time he tried.

And Alma.

Alma, good and natural as wheat. He shook his head. Christ, she was *too* good. Did all a wife could do. Still baked for them from scratch every day. Terrific mother. Yet increasingly the more thoughtful she was, the more obvious her virtues, the more it enraged him. They still screwed—the voice in Randy's head pronounced this word roughly, to distance himself with its deliberate harshness. Gathering her familiar, freckled body to him still a reflex like breathing—but he was embarrassed to find himself newly critical of Alma's appearance. It seemed drab to him, samey. Her hair had started streaking gray—though in fairness, so had his. He found her lacking in something he couldn't quite nail. Wit, imagination, ambition. (These were not qualities it would have occurred to him to require in the days of their dancing and drinking, in the days of cleaning and planting and watching the night sky on the front lawn.) He tried to curb his strange irritation but it found its way out, uglily sometimes, and when it did he could see her expression—like a cell dividing in four, with all the parts struggling silently against each other. He became cruel.

"Don't be such a fucking saint," he heard himself tell her one day. He watched her face, sick with himself. They hadn't spoken the rest of the day.

He'd introduced a contaminant into what had been a guileless marriage, he knew. And he could not face taking steps to rout it.

That contaminant was his chief happiness now.

Randy set the mug on the step, and stood. He dusted his hands, pressed them into his lower back, stooped to collect the mug. Through the screen door he smelled the cheerful residue of fried pancake batter and coffee dregs, heard the sounds of dishes stacking, his daughter's voice singing in high, peaked chanting as she rummaged around, those goofy made-up-on-the-spot songs she favored, that named and linked all she knew. Time to drop her off soon. He would remind Alma he was making the rounds of county officials today—too risky to say he'd be at the office, for she might phone there. And he would drive to Sequoia to the Holiday Inn where a room had been reserved under a name taken from the phone book, a room for which he would pay in cash.

He had always felt a casual contempt for married men who couldn't keep their dicks in their pants. It had been a lowlife occupation, to his thinking—a mark of slovenliness, a colossal waste of time. Self-sabotage. And in bars and other occasions of male conversation he was always skillful in not making a big commotion about it as he quietly turned aside that talk.

Now to learn that, apparently, the impulse had always been in him. All his life, like a dormant cell. Connecting him with a lower order. Waiting for the most offhand prompting.

He watched himself like a movie. One of those old black-and-white silents they showed on Saturday mornings along with cartoons when he was a kid: Harold Lloyd dangling from a giant tower-clock's hand. The clockhand stuck at three. What would happen to poor Harold when the hand slipped down to six? Fascinated now, by the image of himself

hanging by fingertips—over what? Something dark, hopelessly deep, with spikes at the bottom to impale you when
you fell?

He didn't know what he dangled above, and in his mind
there was some reason he could not resist, to wait, watch.

A dog barked twice in the distance.

Only the beginning. Trading one system, its set of simple
parameters, for a more elaborate version. Release now, ela-
tion now, but later—and he sensed this so vaguely it took
form not in words, but as a steady, low tone, like in Alma's
hearing tests—later would come inescapable weight, com-
plexity. Just beginning. Something like being in debt to
the bank, for as long into the future as you could imagine.
Powerless to un-want, Randy could already feel his confines
tighten—the way a mime, his painted-black mouth turned
hugely down in surprised dismay, palms the invisible walls of
his imprisoning cell.

Now it was January of 1987, time for the rains to come, and the Rincon did its duty and rose, pooling at the doorsteps of those who lived too near it. Days were dark, cold. And Leann Hornby lay dying at home.

Alma heard it through Caroline, Big Dave Everton's wife—one of the earth mothers—whom Alma met carrying her plastic basket along the damp, celery-smelling aisles of Jinn's Market.

Alma couldn't at first fathom what Caroline was telling her, grotesque as it was. A brain tumor, discovered far too late. Doctors had declared it too far gone; they could do no more than prescribe drugs to make the child comfortable. Mavis Regan had chosen to bring the girl home to die. Alma listened, engulfed with horror and pity, stricken afresh by the pour of guilty relief—*It wasn't Kira, Kira is safe*—and by her routinely unkind thoughts in the past about Leeann. As if her secret dislike had somehow helped bring about disaster. Caroline was that afternoon going to visit the girl (she had already arranged for a teen-aged sitter to round up and watch her kids). Did Alma wish to come along?

Alma decided at once to go.

Caroline Everton was a big woman with a vast soft shelf of bosom, who always wore a paisley kerchief tied over the crown of her head, knotted under the heavy sheaf of gray-streaked blond hair down her back. She wore long skirts and (depending on the weather) boots or rubber flipflops, oblivious to modern vanities—she never touched makeup or thought about clothing. Yet you would call her striking, and womanly. She had a bold, intelligent nose, penetrating bluegray eyes, good cheekbones, a pensive mouth—altogether a face that telegraphed such kindness and concern it always made Alma want to lay her head in her lap. She had four children of staggered ages with Big Dave, out in the sprawling longhouse Dave had built them in an area called Manzanita, which was then just empty, raw countryside toward the north, remote as a place could be. (Who'd have imagined the retirement suburb, or the billboards advertising it for miles in both directions along the freeway leading through, in twenty years?) The Evertons kept a bunch of animals, including a couple of goats and some chickens, and took in whomever or whatever needed tending. *The original earth mother and proud of it*, Alma would think, admiring Caroline with wistfulness.

Now Caroline had the sad duty of giving Alma the news.

"Poor baby. Just eleven years old. Why they didn't think to get that girl checked earlier, I can't figure—'course it's not," she murmured at once, "my place to say. Should we leave your car here?"

By *they*, Caroline meant Leeann's father, Ed Hornby, and Mavis Regan. But Ed was a rancher in Montana, for God's sake, thought Alma, and for years had had little truck with the girl; apart from rare visits he'd stayed well outside the child's life. Mavis Regan had declared herself a naturopath at about the same time she'd declared her sexual preferences: for some time now, Alma knew, Mavis had dismissed conventional medicine as a scam and a con. But who could have thought straightaway to connect the child's quirky behavior with a tumor? Alma's mind raced up and down a stark hallway of dozens of facing doors, trying every door, rattling the knobs frantically, each door stickily, stubbornly locked. Alma felt her guts sink with the knowledge that it would have been common sense to have the girl checked physically years ago. True, it may not have changed the present course. But not to have tried it until too late! She shook her head slowly. How could Mavis Regan bear it?

In the store Alma shook all the change from her zippered pouch into her palm, hoisted her plastic poncho over her head, and pressed through Mrs. Jinn's squeaky swinging doors, taking giant steps to the phone booth under the eave outside the market. With the rain roaring around the booth she was obliged to shout into the phone. She arranged with her carpool partner that Kira be collected from school and dropped at a friend's house, to await her there. Then she phoned Randy's office.

Alma reached Randy's secretary Linda, a courteous, thoughtful girl who declared he wasn't in at that moment, nor had she been given his schedule today. Did Alma want to leave word?

Alma left word, wondering how her husband would feel when she gave him the news of Leeann. Might it shake him

(she shut her eyes in the phone booth a moment) out of the
queer distance he'd been keeping for some while? In the face
of Mavis's difficulty, Alma's own complaints felt whiny and
niggling. But might this jar him, help him recall, as we all
do with the shock of another's misfortune, how dear and
fleeting their time was? Of course he would probably think
first off, as she had done, *Not Kira, not Kira, thank God.*
Hastily she repented of this line, recoiling at its selfishness.
Again she held her poncho over her head and hurried from
the phone booth into the dark rain, waving an arm to signal
Caroline, who sat waiting in the driver's seat of her old Volks-
wagen bus.

The rain curtained steadily that day, silvergray ropes,
evenly spaced, roaring, perpetual. Like a falls. The cold air
smelled of rivermud, wet leaves. The two women pulled onto
the gravel drive beside Mavis's rented bungalow on Orchard
Avenue, a few blocks from Center. In that '30s neighborhood
each low house was made differently from its fellows—some
gabled and gingerbready, some flat and plain—a feature
which had always charmed Alma. Most had front porches.
A sweet enough place to live, Alma thought, feeling a flit of
abashedness for the size of the house Randy was building
them. This bungalow of Mavis's was just right, she told herself sternly, for two.

And then her heart sank afresh, remembering: one.

It would have to be right for one.

"Where are you?"

With a vigorous bounce Darla propped herself sideways on an elbow, fist supporting her curly head. She tucked the bedsheet over her breasts and under her arms, and looked down at the man on his back beside her. One of his forearms pillowed his neck; the other still grasped the sheet and thin hotel blanket he had yanked up around his chest to conserve the warmth of the two of them. The rain outside came so hard it melted together as one solid pour, in parabolic sheets against the windowglass.

"What's going on in there?" She swiped his brow with a teasing forefinger, the way you might touch cake frosting to pull away a lick. Her gaze was calm and fond.

"Too much," Randy said, his eyes on the ceiling. "Too much going on."

"Crisis?" Her perfume breathed under the warm sheet with them.

"Not exactly."

"What then, exactly?"

He pulled his eyes from the ceiling, which was coated with the stuff that resembled cottage cheese. He looked at her.

"Juggling too much." He didn't say juggling knives.

She smiled. "Simplify."

He snorted. "Easy for you!"

"I'm doing it, aren't I? So it's possible," she said. Her voice was reasonable, light, firm.

"I really can't see how much longer—"

"Baby, we've been through this a thousand times. We're waiting until the kids are a bit older, so they'll be able to handle it."

"And in the meantime?"

"Figure out what doesn't absolutely have to be done, and don't do it," she answered.

Randy made a sound like a horse flapping air from its lips.

"Thanks," he said.

"Baby, you're still in control at work, and with the house-building. There's a word going around at the office, in their corporate memos. *Delegate*. The verb. Meaning—"

"I know what it means."

His head felt compressed at the temples and in his ears, the way it does when you dive into water too deeply, too fast. He laced his hands behind his head, staring up at the cottage cheese.

"I had a college history teacher once," he said.

"Many of us did," she said pleasantly.

"I've forgotten most everything I ever learned from him. Him or anybody else. But I remember something he told our class."

"Yes?"

"'All of history is ultimately a story of what problem needed to be solved, and of who happened to be in a position to attempt to solve it.' Something like that."

She was silent a moment, weighing the advisability of response. She slid down next to him and tucked her arms around him, resting her head on the inside of his upper arm. She ran a manicured hand along his flank: the gentle brush of hair on his thighs stopped exactly midway where his shorts would begin; the skin above that invisible line paler, nude and smooth.

Her voice was quiet.

"What can I do to make it better?"

Her warmth, the incredible softness of the tops of her thighs and breasts, grazed him, then snugged to him. He sighed, stroked her curls.

"Everything and nothing," he murmured.

"You can never have been born. You can never leave me," he said.

She smiled. "I choose the latter." Her eyes held a triumphal sheen.

"C'mere," he said.

But she was already there.

All this occurred a long time ago, remember. I'm making my best attempt to reconstruct it here. I hadn't thought about it, to be honest—hadn't pulled the images from my memory for the longest time. Until I came upon the letter. That was when the story floated back up—but in pieces, you see. I'm trying to arrange them. It's a job, getting the sequence right. It feels as though I am developing some very old film. Give me a little slack, as we say, if the pictures seem to be wearing a veil of smoke.

Do you remember Graham's first girlfriend, Annie Freed?

That was me. I left Graham Payne—oh, but it does seem lifetimes ago—because I had fallen very hard for Bruce Mason, who was a schoolteacher back then. He was just starting out with it. With his gentle good looks and that earnest way of his, Bruce turned me into soup. He was kind of a young Abe Lincoln. So I left poor Graham. We hadn't been happy anyway before I went. I knew he'd been looking at women—well, he'd lost his mother; he was in a certain amount of confusion. Of course, it was Graham's nature to be confused. I was frightened to leave, yes, but I also had a chaotic idea about being brave. Do the young possess any ideas that aren't chaotic? I believed it was a favor to Graham as well as to me, that I go off to find what I thought was missing. I worked awhile at Centurion Equity with Darla Messenger; we knew each other only a little back then—or ever, truthfully. And I did go on to live with Bruce for some years. But soon enough—and perhaps I deserved it, and perhaps I should always be thankful it happened this way—Bruce phoned me at work one sparkling morning and said in a high, strained voice, "I've rented myself a house, Annie." It was a cabin he'd found, actually. Out toward Moreno Bay, just a short walk from the low craggy cliffs that led down to Stone Cove. Abe Lincoln had to take his turn, it seemed, to investigate what *he* felt was missing. A kind of sad daisy chain of missingness, weren't we. After that it did not take me long to comprehend that it would soon be time to leave Ferris.

Oh, I loved our tribe—don't mistake me. But when you consider what was available to a young woman by herself, just then at the brink of life—well, there was nowhere left to take it. Take myself, I mean, inside that circle. Inside Ferris. At least, nowhere I could feature desiring. Do you see? It was the endpoint of that desire. Desire has a shelf life, it seems. Or rather, it mutates. It's mutable. So you spend a goodly portion of your life building up a world around a desire, and then *whoosh*. It's quaint to me now—how in thrall we are to the abstract notion of a thing. Then face to face with it, it has warts, limitations. What's before you is never quite as beautiful as the promise of it in the distance, is it—the idea of the thing you're looking at and guessing about, in the great far away. Artists try and try to get at it, that exquisite unknown, shimmering yonder. Who can blame them?

So there it was. The need to hide away in blue retreat had left me. Maybe we're only fickle creatures. Maybe we have a built-in urge to push the pendulum all the way to the other side, after a certain amount of a thing. Either way, I couldn't put off knowing what I'd sensed for some time: the shabby town that time forgot, set off out there in greenblue pastures and orchards near the sea—blocked off all the different possibilities for me as surely as a medieval city's high stone walls hold off its enemies.

So I moved as far as I could, to the other side of the country.

I worked as a court reporter. I did travel. Many countries. And do you know, everywhere I went I saw people being decent. Doing their best, mostly, to stay upright and make their ways. Don't you think that's something? Now I keep a quiet retirement in this condominium. Low maintenance. A little balcony, a hibachi, a few plants. Sequoia's big enough now to offer anonymity. I'm comfortable. Books, music, a movie sometimes. Peace is the main ingredient here. The only remaining desire.

I am old.

I seldom go to Ferris, though it's just two hours away. What happened exactly during the years after I left, I can never, of course, factually know. But I believe, with a tiredness foisted on me like a medal, that I can imagine it. When I do, the story takes on something of the life I remember. It can't be complete, of course; it won't be perfectly accurate. But we know that even if you and I were never to blink while we watched a boy catch a ball, with no one else around to interrupt or distract—we'd each of us produce two different accounts of it. That's the confounding wonder. Nonetheless I must hammer it out: this mishmash of the imagined married clumsily to memory, with some pieces forever missing. It's important, at least to me, to think it through. A person has to put certain memories in order before she can lay them away. It was the letter, dug up from the boxes of papers I meant to sort, which put the matter before me again.

On a Sunday afternoon in March of 1987, Alma and Randy Winslow stood in the sand at Stone Cove, facing out to sea. Around them, stationed at random intervals facing the same direction, ranged the members of the tribe. Most had left their children at home, though a few carried new babies. They were dressed in what you might call Sunday clothes, though none of these people had seen the inside of a church since they were little, if ever, and the clothes they wore would scarcely have met typical standards for churchwear. The men had combed and neatly tied their hair. The women's faces were scrubbed and unadorned. The group formed a human semi-circle, a sort of bandshell-shape around a lone figure in a space at their center. That figure was Mavis Regan, dressed in a tunic blouse and shorts, and she carried a small, oblong wooden box.

It was cold and windy, and the light had a mottled quality: an overcast sky leaden and close, shot with purple and ochre. The tribespeople looked around at each other. Big Dave and Caroline, Bram Parnell and his new girlfriend Vera, who wore her black hair in two long pigtails. Laurel the dancer, Rex the Adonis. Lane the poet, Sebastian the daredevil doctor.

Graham Payne stood with Darla. Graham's head was lowered. The earth mothers were there, the puppy-like younger
brothers, the mystic, the juggler, the ambulance technician,
and dozens of others. Alma caught sight of old Mrs. Jinn,
 wrapping her nubby purple wool coat tighter, and Mavis
Regan's pharmacy boss, Travis McMurty, a large, pink-cheeked
man in a beige windbreaker, hands folded over themselves
before him. Few spoke. The wind whipped at them.

The water was cold, grayblue of dark metal, with little
spitting whitecaps popping up and dissolving across its surface like gooseflesh. It smelled of seaweed, visible in the shal-
lows like someone's wild hair, loosed and floating near the
surface, a green network of tubes and leaves washing back
and forth in the choppy water.

Alma's eyes ached, partly with the leached light of the
cold afternoon sun and partly from the effort to hold back
the sporadic press of tears, and she wondered whether she
could stick it out. She tried taking Randy's hand, but after
a respectful few minutes he pulled his away. It wasn't something they'd ever quite known how to do—extended hand-
holding. One or both of them would become aware of a
cramped position, a clamminess or an itch, the need to fetch
a tissue or adjust something. Lately Alma found her own
hands, especially her left hand, making an involuntary fist as
she moved through the days. The fist held the thumb at its
center as if in protection, or as if it might be called upon suddenly to hit something. Whenever she became aware she was
doing it, she made an exasperated little noise and opened
both her hands wide; walked around with them way open,
fingers splayed, giving them an impatient shake. Then she'd
forget all about it until she noticed her hands fisting again.

Randy seemed remote, and grim. The occasion would warrant that, but he was always cool these days, never quite in her radar. She wished she could reach for him. Reach him. She hugged herself in the chill.

Randy did not allow himself to look at Alma, at Graham or Darla, or anyone, really, though he'd nodded to people on their way in, whenever a grave pair of eyes caught his. He looked straight out to sea, with the figure of Mavis a blur in the periphery. Randy was thinking that since monstrous things happened for no good reason, it was probably twice as foolish as he already believed it was to imagine there was a pattern or plan, or system of rewards or demerits for the life you lived. Yet a morbid fancy scraped at the edges of his mind with a teeth-vibrating *screek*: if he were ever to lose his daughter, he would assume without question that it had been his punishment. If Kira were suddenly taken the way Leeann had been—he would have no choice but to believe it had been a deliberate, meticulously personal punishment to him. And to finish off that job he'd have to end himself.

As simple as that.

"Friends!"

Mavis Regan had turned to address the tribe. Her face, when Alma glimpsed it, gave Alma a start. It was pale, but radiant. Radiant with belief, the face of Joan of Arc in clips from a silent film that had frightened Alma to death when she was young. Real light seemed to stream from her face, her eyes purged almost white as they lifted. The face of an ecstatic vision. Someone had brought Mavis, for an emergency series of sessions, to a psychotherapist in Sequoia who had studied with Elizabeth Kübler-Ross. The tribe had taken up a hasty collection to pay for the sessions; the therapist had discounted her rate in view of the situation. It was a mercy. Mavis had burned cleanly through her grief.

Or believed she had, thought Alma hollowly. Either way, if it relieved her, even for a time, then God bless the therapist.

Mavis Regan was ready. She talked loudly over the wind, with a lilt and a sureness.

"Friends, I want to thank you for coming to witness. You were all in Leeann's life, and you've all helped me with her."

Alma's hands fisted tightly under her folded arms.

"Now we say goodbye to the spirit of Leeann, which is already on its way, but needs your help to finish the journey. I'll give the ashes of her body back to the earth, by way of the sea. . . . The sea she loved, and where she played."

Mavis held the box with both hands high in front of her, a posture from old Egyptian paintings, bearing offerings. With a girlfriend at either side, each of whom placed a steadying hand at the small of her back, Mavis walked—holding her head, and the little box, high—with the measured steps of a graduate, a bride, toward the cold water.

People moved together gently behind her, to follow her. Faces craned to the left or right of the heads in front of them, to continue to be able to see. Alma felt herself craning, too—and then a great spasm of embarrassment and shame came over her. The entire crowd was rubbernecking, as they might at the scene of an auto accident; their witnessing, so-called, was prurient. These people had no right to be here, Alma thought, no right to be surging behind Mavis this way, all curious eyes, gawkers at a show. *None of us believes whatever it is Mavis is believing right now.* Not really. None of us knows what to believe, she thought. We're voyeurs, titillated.

Still, she could not very well leave now. And it would be grossly disrespectful to speak. Miserable, she tramped slowly through the sand behind the others, following Mavis down to the gray water. Then it occurred to her to move offside of the proceedings, hang back from the others, and let the distance between herself and them widen. At least for herself, she could do this much, she thought. Randy moved along with the others, probably in a trance, unaware she had dropped back.

It was in fact quite difficult to see.

Alma could glimpse, from her stance slightly higher up and to the right on the sloping sand, the figure of Mavis Regan (small as a pinkie finger in Alma's sight) wade waist-high into the choppy cove water with her two friends flanking her. After some moments the two friends backed away from Mavis in separate directions. Mavis faced alone out to sea, continuing to hold her box high. Then Mavis made a series of movements that were difficult for Alma, at that distance, to make out. Alma knew, of course, that Mavis was pulling the lid from the little box and turning the box upside-down, emptying its contents over the water. Then Mavis Regan opened out her arms, lid in one hand and box in the other, the way you would after tossing a bird into the air. Alma saw, very faintly, a thin sideways puff of powder or dust spray itself into the air above the water. It landed light as pollen onto the water, and in less than an instant became part of the dark pocked surface. That little puff seemed so faint. No more than what you blew off the top of neglected furniture.

It made Alma stand stock-still.

In Northern California, the seasons have a delicacy and a character. Many who live here believe that autumn is the region's glory. The sky turns a deep turquoise, light grows fragile, as if made of motes spaced farther apart, and the air is tender, clear, still warm in the fullness of day, cradling the senses. The rows of green vineyards in the flatlands and along the hills, relieved of their prized berries, lapse to dusty gold. The hills themselves are already goldened by summer—earlier a fire hazard, now a plush backdrop—and the trees have all at once burst into red, fanning out in shades of mango, melon, wine. Aspens and birch hang with individually threaded coins, the shiny yellow of new gold; these tremble and glitter in unison as the wind passes.

An absurdity of lavishness. Sunflowers line the fences and garden beds, faces lifted in all directions, heralding. Agapantha sends out geodesic purple spheres. Japanese maples' miniature leaves become dark opals. Pumpkins swell to boastful sizes in scattered rows along the topsoil. Sometimes a truck loaded high with them can be seen rolling its brilliant orange mound through the center of town and onto the highway, to the waiting world. Out come the flannel shirts in bright plaids, the mufflers, the boots; out come the cider stands and grade-school paper cut-outs, silhouettes of witches and pilgrim hats taped to walls, windows. Scents of sharp woodsmoke snake about. The animals smell these changes, alert and quickened, and the people in the town move among each other with a heartiness, and behind that, a pang. The season wills, and we obey. Everything works together in a last hotsweet flare before the dark winter rains cover it, melting away the blazing costumes, putting it all to sleep.

Autumn is a fraught time. People in the best of circumstances turn inward, take measure, feel something wanting. But Graham Payne was so accustomed to this frame of mind that the mood of the season caused no major shift in him. Graham moved through his duties, carrying out his appraiser work (it suited him), shuttling Ethan to school, soccer practice, clarinet. Darla was not the same, and had not been the same for a long time. She was brisk and businesslike; not coy and doting as she had been when they started out. It dismayed him, but he did not act. He had no sense of an occasion for taking action. And whether it came from his nature or his fear of rupture, his absorption of dismay was unthinking, the way you pick up a stray bit of crumpled paper and drop it in a wastebasket. He ascribed Darla's difference to her growing status at work. She'd been made a senior vice president, forever called to vital meetings, sessions with big clients; sometimes for several days to various hub cities. My God, the *clothes* she'd acquired. Graham believed Darla was always years ahead of him in understanding, and delivering, what the world required. That was her gift.

He moved along in a mulling state.

Leeann Hornby's death had pushed a little crater into Graham's heart that would not punch back out, and even three-and-a-half years later the sadness rode around with him. He'd never much liked the kid, but that counted little against the imponderable fact of a child's death. The sudden non-being of a child, the dumb space where personality and light and energy had been—was more shocking to him, more an offense against nature, than the negation of an adult. It was the closest he'd been to such willy-nilly violence, except for the loss of his mother—though it seemed a sly relation to that loss.

Graham walked, thinking, one long hand on his son's shoulder, across the trampled grass of the Commons, among giant square bales of pungent hay. These served as sales tables for the Harvest Fair, something Ferris did every year the weekend before Halloween. Most of the townspeople and a stream of out-of-towners had shown up, either as customers or hawkers of the usual treats: earrings and bead bracelets, loaves of fresh bread, pastries, cakes, raw walnuts and almonds, gallons of homemade juice and cider, beer and wine. A country group played fiddle. The hay bales created a small maze of avenues, along which purveyors offered their wares. Face-painting, hair-braiding, carved birdhouses, little framed watercolors. Bram Parnell proudly manned his own hay bale this year, with Vera standing by as his assistant: his sketches displayed on miniature easels, handbound books of his cartoons stacked to either side. Smells of the fair made your saliva work: smoked sausage, steamed corn on the cob, charcoal-baked potatoes, heavy clam chowder, burritos. Spit-roasted turkey legs, yeasty ale. Among these aromas, the river sent up its muddy scent, twined with a saline whiff of the bay. The Saturday afternoon held champagne light, the air a champagne snap.

Ethan Payne was twelve years old. His body—doughy at the middle, large of hands and feet, slendering at the shins and shoulders—seemed paused in one long gathering moment before it shot to stunning height. He had thick, dark hair, olive skin, eyes so dark they shone black, and a face that combined his parents' features. His mouth was sensuous, his brow very serious. Today Ethan tramped along beside his father, eyeing the trinkets and bottles and books with controlled impatience. He was more interested, lately, in mountain bikes. Fortunately for Ethan, all the boys his age in Ferris happened to feel the same way, and an enterprising tribe member named Bayard Avery, noting this, had recently opened a bicycle business called Roundabout. He'd set up a demonstration area to one side of the hay bales.

"Dad, look! The bike shop!" Ethan strode ahead of Graham, whose guiding hand dropped away as his son's shoulder sped forward.

Graham's lips lifted in a vague smile. He liked seeing Ethan's attention swept up, so that at least for the moment the boy would lose his habitual frown. Graham never considered for a moment that his own face might echo the boy's. In truth there was a difference. Graham's was milder, humbler, more receiving. Ethan's frown was on its guard, leery. Graham watched him join a dozen other boys around several shining models—metallic blue, emerald, purple, candy-apple frames with extra-thick tread tires; spokes and wires glinting silver. The kids asked Bayard Avery questions; he answered them with amused patience. They exclaimed to each other as they ran their hands over the models. Graham watched Ethan squatting to check a price tag tied to a silver spoke. *Christmas*, Graham was musing as he approached the excited group. Well, one less decision. It simplified things.

And that was when Graham crashed directly into Randy Winslow, who was crossing (striding too fast, eyes glassily preoccupied) from one of the intersecting lanes created by the piled haybales. They collided at some speed.

"Whoa!"

"Ow! Hey!"

"Hey—Randy."

"Graham."

The two men recovered themselves, embarrassed. They faced each other and shook hands: one tall and loose and long-faced, one compact and tense. Sometimes they looked away as they talked, sometimes at the hay-strewn ground. From a mild distance, they could have been talking about lawn mowers, or roofing costs. Had you been standing near them, pretending to look at the scented candles or the bamboo flutes, you would have heard this exchange:

"How you doing, bro."

"Doing fine, bro, fine. You?"

"Doing okay. Doing okay. What's going on? How's Alma? Kira? That house finished now?"

"Oh, Alma's good, thanks. Yeah, we finally moved into the house. S'a good thing, man; we were getting crowded out there. Oh, Kira's great. Kira's great. And, uh—Darla? Ethan? That Ethan over there?"

"That's him. Bike fever. Gotta make him wait 'til Christmas for it, though. Darla's good, fine. She's senior VP now over at Centurion, you know."

"She is?"

"Yeah. Promoted like crazy. About to rule the universe, I guess."

"No kidding. Hah. That's great. That's great."

Pause.

"You get any surfing in anymore?"

"Nah. Up to my ears in work. Pathetic. You?"

"Nah. Too much going on."

"Yeah. Same for me."

"Randy, do you—"

Graham paused a fraction of a beat.

"Do you remember the porpoises? That day we sat out waiting for sets at the Cove?"

"Do I! Oh, man, sure I do, Graham. Of course I do. Wasn't it the best."

"It was, bro. The very best. I don't think—don't think I'll ever forget it."

"Me neither. No way. . . ."

A pause.

"Man, Ethan's looking good, Graham. Big now. Lot like both of you."

"Yeah. Ethans's a good kid. A good boy."

The two men stood another moment.

"Graham, I hate to run away, but I'm late for an interview—we're hiring more staff, see, and I really gotta—"

"No, that's fine, Randy. Fine. Really. Good to see you again. Been too long, eh? Maybe we could—do something soon."

"Yeah. Yeah, we should. Maybe find some more waves again one of these days."

"I'd love that. I really would. Hey, give my best to Alma and Kira."

"Yeah, sure, thanks and—uh, me too, to your guys."

"Sure."

"Take care, now."

"Take care."

That is the way men talk to each other, or at least the way most men did back then. What they feel or think, that's another matter. Graham stood watching Randy leave. He knew Randy had soared past him in ambition and achievement, and almost certainly made better money. But this part didn't bother Graham so much. What Graham most felt was a kind of bereftness. How could there ever have been a time such as both men remembered, when the two had had nothing more on their minds than praying for good surf conditions, or anticipating the first beer's cold, biting tang at day's end? How often he longed to return to that feeling! How spacious it now seemed: clean and light, simple as slipping into a pair of shorts on a warm summer morning. He had forgotten, as most of us do, the angst that had spurred him in those days. Spurred many of us back then. Pressing, pressing its murmured demand into the mind daylong, all those years: *What am I supposed to be doing? What is to become of me?*

Randy stalked blindly from the fair. He took the walkway and then the dirt path to the river, stood under a canopy of firs and eucalyptus. He watched the brown water. The Rincon was running low, made a pleasant trickling sound, and smelled cool and muddy under the trees. Behind him at some distance, the noise of the fair. A white heron lifted straw- legs, poking at silt along the bank. Randy looked at the bird without seeing it or thinking "bird," his hands stuffed in his pockets. He tried to take a few deep breaths, but his chest wouldn't open. Randy had seen Graham's face and heard his words, seen Graham's sad haplessness, his trust in the ambient structure of his life. And Randy saw at once why Graham drove Darla to distraction, as she had complained. At the same time he felt stricken by it, that she should revile Graham for being Graham. He'd felt Graham's nostalgia for the friendship the two men had lost. Graham had fairly held it out in his hand to Randy, like a long-lost boot he'd just found.

A boot with no mate.

And Randy had glimpsed the boy Ethan. It had been some years.

Unwitting stepson. Readymade.

"Sweet fucking Jesus," he whispered to the river.

The afternoon the two old friends collided, Darla Messenger Payne took a bath.

It was a rare opportunity. Between the insurance game and family duty and seeing her lover, she was a woman on wheels. Baths are the last real luxury, she thought, watching the steaming line of hot water rise against the porcelain. She reached for the bath salts; watched the blue crystals glint, little faceted jewels under the column of water. It was a glorious afternoon, a stillness and purity in the autumn air. Pachelbel on the stereo. She liked that *Canon in D* everybody was so wild about. It seemed to be the sound of ceremony: stepping forward in a slow, serene way, counting steps. One, two, three, four. Measuring progress. When the music stopped you'd know precisely where you stood, how much ground had been covered. One, two, three, four. Turn off the water. Stepping in. Easing down. Oh.

No feeling quite like it. Up, up to the collarbone. Let the hair get wet; I'll wash it after.

All was well. All was being managed, moving forward by increments. Darla took the loofah and began to soap her slender arms. She often felt like one of those chess champions who roves from table to table, studying each board, and after extended moments—deducing, adducing, running options and consequences—picks up her token and places it. Then on to the next board, the next table.

Darla had taught herself, above all things, not to waste time. Complaining wasted time. So did self-pity. So did indecision, dithering. Her instincts to swiftly cut away obstructions had been molded by watching her lawyer father, of course, but she'd stropped these instincts shiny and blade-keen, working in Ferris. Actually, it wasn't technically Ferris she worked in any longer. Centurion Equity was New York-based; its branch offices honeycombed the state, and the Ferris office was but a satellite. Since being named an executive officer for the western division, her skills were required across an immense territory. If a client in Houston or Spokane or Phoenix decided to change coverage, it was Darla's task to fly out and design a plan to fit (and to profit Centurion, of course). This meant carrying every inch of herself in a way that spelled *solution*, so her clients would relax and cooperate. It meant looking fabulous. She smiled at the tiny gold hairs laying wet along her forearm. Looking fabulous had never hurt a client relationship yet. But no businessman dared smirk at Darla. A few had tried; they'd soon revised their misperceptions. Darla had a handshake that could cause pain, and an eyegleam and speaking manner that told nervous executives two things. She would not fail them, and she would never, ever be fooled.

The water was very hot, the way she preferred it. Scented steam, the scent of freesia, opened the pores of her skin. The light through the bath window's frosted glass was soft as fog.

She ran the loofah around her neck, behind her ears, over her slim shoulders. In the main Darla charmed people, and bouquets of flowers awaited her at contract signings, planning sessions. Lunches, too, were gracefully choreographed to leave warm impressions in everyone's belly along with the pricey food. Whenever she could, Darla found a way to meet Randy in some of the cities she serviced, as well as in Sequoia. Her reward for this strategizing finesse was a growing bank account, the beauty of her son, the deliciousness of her lover.

The peace of a solitary bath.

She lifted a brown leg (amid a rich *plosh* of water), and admired its shapeliness. Lazily she scrubbed a heel.

It was perhaps odd, but no one's business if she chose to keep Randy screened off until Ethan was fifteen. She would not have the child exposed to the upheaval of divorce until he was at least that old. It was unfortunate she couldn't have started up with Randy later in time, but it simply hadn't worked that way, and besides, there was something exciting about the challenge of the masquerade, the logistics of the game (she bit a lower lip, soaping arches and the tops of painted toes)—an energy. She took particular nourishment from it, though she would never have admitted this if asked.

Randy was unhappy and nervous about it, but they drank of each other—she thought of the painted wallpaper she'd seen in one restaurant, a bacchanale scene in which nymphs and satyrs emptied goatskins of wine into each other's mouths, gamboling between olive trees. Everyone in moist disarray, beaming rosily at each other. (Randy was, she thought, like an expensive sauterne: clear, pale, heady.) Not least, Randy contained what she most missed in Graham. Purpose. Power. Randy went after what he wanted, and he wanted plenty. He did not pause to debate, to anguish, to doubt as Graham did, and my God, she was sick of tending Graham's doubts. Everyone has a nature that takes shape in a gesture. She was molded of the will to strike, to strike forth. Randy was like her. When she and Randy combined forces as husband and wife, there'd be nothing they couldn't do, nothing they couldn't get. And they'd look completely fabulous doing and getting it.

She lifted the second leg, water splashing from it as it rose. She pointed a long foot, and eyed the curvature of the foot's arch, the sleekness of her calves. It was to her credit that she'd kept her figure after Ethan, who'd been an inordinately big baby, but she'd always known she couldn't afford not to. She applied the loofah: heel, toe, and knee. It would be difficult at first getting Alma and the daughter squared away, and Graham and Ethan. But she would simply pin the marker on the map, and they'd all get there. She would give special attention to Ethan. He was gifted, gorgeous. He'd be a star; she would help him. The children would learn to commute between households; a common enough '90s happenstance. Alma would have to find her way. Hordes of women did it every day. Darla hadn't much to go on in her thinking about Alma, because Randy refused to talk at length about her. He seemed to believe it invasive, and Darla had no wish to force him; likely she'd have been bored or depressed by it anyway. And so she did not dwell on Alma. She knew only that Alma could not be the sum of what Randy needed—because of Randy's passion for Darla herself. If she had helped that passion along, if she played to it—what of that? It was no mystery what the man needed. Stand on a mirror, naked, and look down. That is what men need.

Graham, too, would find his way. She turned onto her belly with a great upheaval of water, laying her cheek against the warmed smoothness, crossing her heels behind her. Warm water enwrapped and floated her. Heaven. (Pachelbel was over. A mockingbird in the jacaranda outside announced its position in a polished eight-note melody, over and over.) Graham would be wounded. There would be trauma, sadness. She sighed, lay her other cheek against the white porcelain. An ordeal. But Graham had never been able to push past some sorrow she could never appease, even if she'd wanted to. And she'd given up wanting to. When she'd determined to marry him, he had not seemed a bad bet. But his mother had willed all the property to his uncle, and the years between had taught her it was not in Graham's character to want to go out and make serious money. Graham, it occurred to her, was more like Ferdinand the Bull, in the children's story Ethan used to insist she read him again and again. Ferdinand didn't want to be chosen to fight in the bullring. He wanted to lounge in the meadow under a cork tree and sniff flowers. Ferdinand's mother allowed him this because she adored him. All very sweet for a child's story, but not—she closed her eyes, sighed again—not for the functions of a modern husband. And she wasn't Graham's mother.

Of course, that was the ultimate mistake of it. What he'd needed her to be.

Abruptly Darla turned back over, gathered her pretty legs under her and pushed herself up, rising, rising from the water with a great noisy pouring of it from all sides of her, like Venus being born.

It was about a year after Leeann's death that Mavis Regan decided to learn flamenco.

Many parents do surprising things after a child dies. I read of one woman somewhere who joined a sex club. Mavis wasn't interested in that route. It's true she was seen from time to time with a girlfriend, but people learned to be careful not to ask directly how Patty or Shambhala was—it was bound to put Mavis in a scowling funk. The girlfriend issue, in that time and region, was problematic for Mavis. Because of logical trends of migration (starting in the city and ranging out, by cautious degrees, toward the country), gay culture had not yet gained a foothold in Ferris, California. So Mavis Regan was obliged to seek most of her girlfriends at two or three bars in Sequoia. These women were pleasant enough, but often, in Mavis Regan's own words, they were "not the brightest bulbs." This peeved Mavis Regan, because she felt she deserved, as she put it, "to be met."

Mavis had always felt a curiosity about flamenco, though until then she'd had almost no exposure to it. She'd seen the Jose Greco troupe on television shows when she was a kid. After she was grown she would occasionally catch a glimpse of the dance as part of something else, often as the background in a movie. But these depictions tended to be fleeting. Then on one of her trips to Sequoia, walking along Robles Street toward the Home Helper hardware store, she had overheard the syncopated clapping and the *allegro*, the peppering clatter of hard shoe heels striking a wooden floor. She'd followed the sound up the external stairs of what appeared to be an old warehouse into a doorway. And found a studio.

She'd signed up that afternoon. Twice a month Tuesdays, she drove her old Subaru to the city. She wore a black leotard top and leggings, and tied a length of floral-print cloth around her waist.

What drew Mavis to the dance was its furious power. She thought she'd never seen anything so rawly soulful. The men and women seemed to be fueled by something that came up from the center of earth straight through the bottoms of their feet. The best dancers seemed to be investigating a question, or a problem. They melted away the irrelevant parts of themselves to an essence—like wicks of a flame, burning white—as they followed the question inward and down, round and round. As the dark music wailed the dancer's arms rose slowly, up and back, high and arched, like an aroused serpent. The back arched, the head held tall with angry pride, sometimes a kind of embattled imploring. The brows knotted—ironic, haughty, tormented. These attitudes seemed to demand that the dancer pursue them: they would lead her somewhere. The torso was the first to turn toward the thing being investigated. Shoulders and hips followed. Head last. Feet stamped out a narrative: thoughtful, stronger, finally exploding. A secret spiral staircase, twisting and twisting, deeper in, deeper down. A human corkscrew. The closer the dancers got to the center of the question, the more something else began taking over. Something invisible. A kind of animus or spirit. When it did, the dancer became possessed, and the body could hardly move fast enough—smacking itself across chest and hips, hurling the arms straight up and down, the background singers hailing: *Vaya, Olé!*

Mavis had learned, from her teacher, that the animus had a name. *Duende.* It only entered those who'd worked long, with purity of purpose, at the dance. Even Mavis Regan, queen of irreverence, knew not to throw that word around cavalierly.

"Come with me. Watch us," she said to Alma Winslow one morning in the old plaza square. Mavis was on her way to the Merit pharmacy job, which she had decided not to leave, because Mr. McMurty had been so kind to her during Leeann's death. He'd given her paid time off, and more hours and benefits, and a raise after she returned. She had also decided not to "abet the enemy," as she phrased it, by going over to the new mall, which she had inspected and indignantly pronounced "plastic."

Mavis had been leveled by Leeann's death, but not emptied.

Alma still shopped at Merit and at Jinn's, out of some dogged loyalty to the old feeling, from the beginning days, of setting up life with Randy. But the businesses were struggling, since three new malls competed now for the shopping dollars of Ferris. The two women stood in the crumbling plaza square, on a cold Monday morning in March of 1992. Kira was a freshman at Ferris High, Alma told Mavis. Leeann had been dead ten years—almost the same length of time she'd managed to live, Mavis mused to Alma.

Alma looked at her. Mavis was older. Her hair had wisps of gray around the edges. But her eyes, though pale, and with little lines radiating out from the corners, retained some of their former flash. She was still not above shooting those needles of sarcasm into people's necks when the moment moved her. No one took offense anymore. By then Mavis was such a fixture in the community, the aging tribe members were actually relieved to find this sign of stubborn life in her.

Mavis had taken Alma by surprise, as usual.

"Come with you? Wouldn't I—be in the way, or make people self-conscious?"

She couldn't quite feature the idea—it was like being asked to a costume party, and she'd be the one in streetclothes. In her right arm she hefted a bag of groceries; her free left hand gripped its thumb in a fist. In a few seconds her awareness of the fist zigzagged to consciousness: she opened the hand and gave it a shake.

"Doesn't your class need its privacy?"

"Naw. I want you to see this. It's something no one should go through life without seeing, at least once. We're having a guest teacher this time, a dancer from Madrid. Born in Granada. Eva's her name. She's been in films and competitions all over the world. C'mon, Alma. You'll never be the same. You'll thank me for it, dolly. I promise."

Mavis cocked her head, narrowed her eyes: a gentle dare. Still prodding people to Grow with a capital G, thought Alma. At least her eyes were more amused than mocking nowadays.

Alma smiled tiredly. She so seldom got out of town.

"Oh, hell, Mavis Regan. Why not."

The two women arrived at the external staircase at the base of the building the following afternoon, and could hear the guitarist as they mounted the metallic steps. The warehouse was plain, just as Mavis had described it; you'd never know from the outside it contained a dance studio. Rent was probably extra low, thought Alma, puffing up behind Mavis—because the neighborhood was grim. Industrial warehouses, weedy lots, rusting pipes, cracked factory-style windows covered with dirt. The early afternoon light was still weak, and it was chilly. The women entered a wide, empty room with (miraculously) a hardwood floor. One wall of ceiling-to-floor mirrors. The rest, plain stucco. Light filled the room from the glass panes along the top of one wall. A folding chair at the back held a funky hi-fi and tape deck system—the guitarist they'd heard, performing *solearas*—with connecting wires to two speakers. Three other folding chairs waited—perhaps for the teacher, her guests. The studio was freezing.

"It'll warm up fast enough once we get started, I promise," Mavis told her.

Alma sat in one of the empty chairs, pulling her parka closer around her.

Driving out of the city, the women were jubilant. Alma was glassy-eyed, babbling.

"Mavis Regan, I swear to you that was the most—that was the most amazing thing I think I have ever seen."

"See, dolly? Did I lie to you? Do I lie to anyone? Could you believe the way Eva moved? The expression on her face?"

"No, Mavis. I will never, never forget it. It will never leave me."

Alma had sat in wonder as the class was led through master paces by Eva Villanueva, a brunette of 34 whose fierce beauty seemed smelted. The moving platoon of dancers advanced upon themselves as a unit in the mirror, arms arched high, hands and fingers twisting, eyes boring, pitiless, into their own reflections, heels hitting the wood in perfect unison—with no music at all but the fearsome silence echoing between their pounding reports. Not a spectacle that quits the mind easily. Alma had pressed her cold hands between her thighs, and stared as if at an air squadron bombardment, hardly breathing. Her heart was still slowing down.

"Mavis, I'll never be the same. Really, I do owe you for this."

"Don't be silly, doll; you don't owe me a blessed farthing. But now you know," Mavis intoned, like a priest, "what I've been yammering about all this time. What keeps my pilot light lit. Now you know."

"Now I know. Believe me. Mavis, do you think that someday I could possibly—hey."

Alma had twisted her head around suddenly, and held it turned, staring behind her through Mavis's smeary rear window.

"Wasn't that Randy's van?"

Mavis tossed a glance at the rear mirror, scanning to the right of the highway. It was an especially unattractive section of frontage road such as frequently limns certain California cities: treeless, brown (dried fields spreading out behind), studded with low storage lockers and rental car lots—and row upon row of commuter motels. Ramada, Holiday Inn. The late afternoon light rendered it bleaker still.

"Where? Where do you see it?" Mavis squinted into the mirror for a glimpse of Randy's silver Lexus van. The silver bullet, Kira called it.

"We just passed it. Ramada parking lot," Alma said.

It was about four o'clock. She racked her memory. Randy was to have attended a board meeting for the center this afternoon, a meeting he'd said might run late—mentioned it this morning. But board meetings always took place in the center offices, in Ferris.

What on earth would he be—

"Can we turn around and just check, please, Mavis?"

"You got it, dolly," Mavis answered in a resolute boom, like a trucker.

She was already signaling, cranking her graying head around to check the lane behind her to the right, changing lanes in time to head for the exit ramp.

Now it is time to talk about Alma Collier Winslow's life until that moment.

Alma maintained a habit of making the best of what was there. She could not honestly remember doing prolonged battle with people or circumstance, having encountered little need for it. Instinctively, she had always found ways to ride out difficult situations like a demure bus passenger, until the next stop—when she would quietly, politely disembark. As a girl (the middle child of three) in San Rafael, then a community of vegetable gardens and small farms, her cooperative nature gratified parents and friends. Who wouldn't enjoy such a girl? Her dependability, her freckled, smiling rejoinder "no problem," made her an ideal choice for babysitting, and caring for people's animals and yards. Alma pitched in. At home, she uncomplainingly performed her chores and errands. At school, she was a staple of student body elections and bake sales. In athletics she'd run track—relay races—and won a ribbon or two. When she made her way to Ferris after two years of community college, she had no expectations of changing her own character. Alma pitched in.

She took pleasure now in her flourishing daughter. Kira was a willowy, contained girl whose wavy hair—the color of pewter—streamed behind her shoulders like a cape. She was a serious student who loved her studies, had close friends, took fencing lessons, played Bach's Two- and Three-Part Inventions on the piano, and arose to each day with a thoughtfulness and poise that baffled Alma.

Where did it come from, that deliberate, unflappable cool? Alma would marvel. In fairness, Randy had always been steady during their setting-up days. Come to think of it, he'd never stopped being sure of whatever he was about. In the workday world he was perceived as a rock, though at home with her he might be distracted and put off. Alma assumed the trait—the confidence gene—was passed along to their daughter by Randy. She was forgetting who she had been in her own girlhood, and during the early days with Randy: cleaning, gardening, baking, dancing, drinking beer. She had been Alma who smiled and worked and smiled. A cheery, pliant soldier. Nothing had fazed her. Hauler of horse manure, dweller in sawdust and nail-studded boards. Nurse, coach, bearer of refreshments. Yet whatever it was she had foreseen starting out, whatever sense of endgame, of relaxing after harvest amid the voluptuous fruit—home, daughter, money—that sense of arrival, so long anticipated it was assumed, had failed to appear. The evidences of success all about her seemed agreeable enough but somehow neutral, incidental, like scenery, while inside her, over past years, something quietly withered. It had happened so subtly and slowly that she had ceased to connect it directly with Randy's slow removal from her.

Since the days of his turning away, she had little by little given up reaching for him. She told herself that this was the way people lived as they aged: a coolness settled over them, a language so minimal it might be taken by an outsider for code. Alma visited with her women friends from time to time, at parties or in the Commons. She laughed with them and traded stories, mainly about the achievements of their almost-grown children. She was grateful for that. But the smile on her face felt taut. She felt it fade too quickly once out of their sight, and she knew what her face must look like once the taut smile vanished: the face of an actor, slumping after the show in her dressing room. She knew, without being able to name it, that something had been skimmed off. Something unnameable had gone missing. And that huge missingness itself hurt her, like a hard object caught in the esophagus. Sometimes she wandered the rooms of the house simply staring at things—furniture, photographs—as if their shapes and surfaces held a solution to the malaise. As though, if she stared long and hard enough, they would open like an armoire and reveal an answer. Sometimes she lay in bed mornings after Kira and Randy were gone. (Randy was always careful to slip noiselessly from the bedclothes.)

She could not think of a single reason to make herself get up.

She did love the big wooden house full of light, and loved the land, the French intensive garden with its fluffy raised beds, and her flowers and vegetables. The hearing-test job was rote by now. But none of these seemed quite the point anymore, if they had ever been the point. Perhaps once they had. She wasn't sure, lately, what the point was. She felt confused and exhausted, and desperately lonely.

Then she'd met Mavis Regan at the old plaza square, and gone to see the electrifying dance with Mavis. And found Randy's car.

Alma had asked Mavis to let her off and wait for her near
the parked silver van. Stepping quickly to it, Alma tried the
doors. They were locked. She cupped her hands around her
eyes to peer through the windowglass. The glass was cool; her
breath made little crescents of steam. The van was Randy's.
She recognized the commuter cup in its slide-out holder, the
black three-ring time management binder, the towel, Kira's
balled-up gym socks, familiar personal debris of his comings
and goings. She crossed the parking lot, entered the lobby of
the Ramada, and asked where the Ferris senior center board
meeting was being held. She was told that no conferences or
meetings were scheduled that day. Then she asked for Randy
by name, but the clerk claimed he had no one registered
there under the name she cited. She insisted there had to be:
he was her husband, and there was his car—she turned to
point through the lobby window—with his things inside, in
the hotel lot fronted by the freeway.

Mavis Regan, waiting and watching in the Subaru wagon
beside the van, seemed to decide something, and turned off
her engine.

The clerk—only a young boy, probably still in high
school—lifted and poked among the papers before him and,
looking at Alma somewhat queerly, asked her to please wait
in the lobby while he called the manager for help. In some
minutes the hotel manager appeared, a thin man with a
sallow complexion, wearing tortoise-shell glasses. He moved
to uncover an oversized album, tilted his head slightly back,
and proceeded to flick through its pages, studying them
through the bottom half of his bifocals, one page after the
next, pulling them rapidly aside and placing his hand against

the examined pile as he did so. Alma knew that many hotels registered their customers' car makes and license plate numbers. She watched, during what seemed both an eternity and a single quivering beat, as the manager finally turned his back to her after pressing a couple of buttons on the front desk phone console. In a moment he lowered his head and put a hand over one ear. She heard his voice speaking very low, but she could not make out the words.

At this time Alma's conscious thoughts had ceased to operate in the sauntering way to which most of us are accustomed, whereby the mind orders its chatter casually and reviews it from time to time with unhurried disinterest—the way you might leaf through a nearby magazine in the course of a dragging day. Instead her thoughts had condensed to a thin, vibrating neon line on a black screen. The line was concentrated, bright, shuddering at little reverberating points and making a high-pitched sound, a test-pattern sound at a piercingly loud, high pitch. Her heart, too, was behaving in an irregular way. It was thumping hard in a shallow but accelerated rhythm, and she felt a creeping numbness in her fingers and wrists, and around her ass where she'd been perched at the edge of the lobby chair. She jumped up as the manager walked out through a little gate at the front desk. He looked at her.

"Your—the owner of the car is coming to the lobby immediately," he said.

But by the time Randy had pushed through the glass entrance door into the lobby, Alma was gone.

In the following years, four events rocked the remaining members of the original tribe of '70s transplants to Ferris, California.

Sebastian Lieber, the daring young physician, died from a hang-gliding accident in 1992. He'd been blown back against a sheer cliff face—up the coast, near Mendocino—the face of the cliff off which he'd sailed. It had broken him like a bird. In the hospital room Sebastian had gazed shrewdly at his caretakers from among his tubes and monitoring machines.

"I'm not gonna make it," he told them softly. "I know it."

His father, a tool-and-die tycoon, flew in from Cologne, Germany to claim the body. Mr. Lieber declined to speak, or have any dealings, with any of Sebastian's former friends. (Poor Sebastian. What must he have fled?) So all the tribe members assembled to hold a separate service for him at an area now called the Rural Cemetery, an overgrown little hill not far from the Commons, preserved by the county as an historical marker—where the earliest town settlers had buried their dead. Some of the stone markers' inscriptions had been worn away by weather and years. Others were quite visible, bearing inevitable messages and commemorations of fathers, mothers, wives and husbands, babies, children. Lane the poet, who had long been Sebastian's lover, read the eulogy he had composed, which included excerpts from Whitman, Stevens, and Santayana. Lane wore Sebastian's red St. Louis Cardinals cap, yanked down hard against the unseasonable August wind. He looked like a Roman emperor wearing a baseball cap.

"And I scarce know which part may greater be," he concluded in a brave, projecting voice with only the slightest quaver. His eyes found the bluegreen line of the hills beyond the town, above and behind the heads of his listeners.

"What I keep of you, or you rob from me."

Two other events that sent shock waves through the Ferris tribe were, of course, the divorces of the Winslows and the Paynes. These took a year to be finalized, during which people were careful not to probe. The children appeared to keep on track with their trajectories in school, though each wore a more serious air than they had in the past. Ethan was to live with his mother, and Kira, with encouragement from Alma, would live with her father. They would visit alternate parents on a regular schedule, to be agreed on by all the parties. Alma made plans to travel to the Pacific Northwest, to visit Oregon friends. Graham rented, at first, an efficiency apartment. (A bloc of these had sprung up, artlessly, along Center Street, at the corner where the old car showroom had been.)

Graham hardly knew what had hit him. The loss seemed a revisitation, in different form, of his mother Vivian's protracted death from cirrhosis. He lived inert for some months in the apartment's bare rooms with a stack of cardboard boxes, as though he had been thrown there by a time machine set to the wrong era. He didn't eat. His breath was bad. Nearly every night he dreamed of his mother's final days: the gray world of it—him going in and out of her bedroom, her gray color and druggy cries for assistance, his uncle Winston's prowling the silent, musty house, addressing Graham with false heartiness even as Winston's fleshy, mustached face sagged with the reality of the situation. Graham would wake gasping and sweaty, and then he would have to cry. He might not have survived this period at all had not a beautiful fairy—akin to the luminous one in *Pinocchio*—stolen in to lead him to safety. It was Laurel, the dancer. No one knows exactly when or how Laurel appeared to Graham, but one day people began to notice the mysterious young woman with him, and thereafter all the time: her sylph's hand swallowed in his long paw, slowly walking the beach at Moreno, or having quiet breakfast in Marlene's. Graham appeared becalmed when he was with her, more reflective. Fixing him with steady graygreen eyes, Laurel listened to him, took him on hikes, made him tea. She was to keep Graham alive, tend him until he could stand up. After a time, Graham did stand up—and moved in with her. They are still living together. Laurel gives dance lessons, and Graham does his appraising. Sometimes he slips into the back row of the darkened auditorium (part of the new Ferris arts complex) during one of her recitals. She dances in cloud-colored material, to Satie, to Sinatra, and watching her, Graham becomes very still.

And Alma. Let us go back to look at her.

She let Mavis drive her home after leaving the Ramada.

The women scarcely spoke the entire two-hour drive. Mavis wisely kept silent. She'd observed for years that Alma was unmet—Lord, the woman's loneliness fairly emanated from her pores. Mavis had also long worried privately for Graham Payne, who struck her as nakedly vulnerable, far more than most adults, unshielded. But Mavis kept silent. People had to come to their reckonings, she was convinced, in their own times and ways. Alma remembers only the dropping afternoon sun, coalesced and magnified through the car windshield, pouring into her left ear. The unexpected warmth was soothing, like oil drops, like a mother's cheek. She felt sleepy. She told herself, in the stupidity of that afternoon, that the sun in her ear was God, or the cosmos, talking to her. *Alma, Alma.*

When she entered the house she wandered from room to room—known to her, yet not known. Without thinking she sat down at the dining table, the three woven placemats with red Peruvian llama designs in their usual positions, crumbs from the morning's muffins still littering them, a scribbled note on Kira's looseleaf notepaper alongside. Hands empty in her lap, she stared out the window. The evening was steeping through, teal-to-ink. The first star winked on. A dove murmured outside. The cold breath of the surrounding hills had permeated the rooms, the heat not yet on, no fire built. Kira's note on the table reminded her parents that she was at fencing class, and going for food afterward with friends; she had a late ride home.

When Randy burst in, Alma was still sitting in the same position in the darkened, cold house. She looked at him mildly. There was no feeling in her hands and feet. Her hands still lay cold in her lap, still as stones but—she noticed slowly, as if from a great height—they lay open.

Randy flicked on the lights. He looked to have just dismounted from a galloping horse. He was flushed and damp, and his eyes shone with witless adrenalin.

"It's cold in here," he said. Angry. The cold, the context. Inevitable, absurd, dreaded so long. He strode to push up the thermostat. The soft click of the forced-air heater acknowledged his command.

"How long," she asked quietly.

Preternaturally calm. A cleanly-snapped bone.

"A long time," he said in a noisy exhale, throwing his canvas briefcase aside.

"Months? Years?"

"Years."

Years.

"Who," she said then.

The heater started up its thick humming. The musty smell of it briefly swiped at their nostrils. How utterly still the house seemed, even with the thrumming of the heated air. She would remember its stillness. A held-breath house, as if someone had died.

"Darla Payne," he answered. He sat on the couch, clasped his hands over his knees.

Alma's eyes swarmed with the first images.

"Why," she said after a few moments. Her voice was dull, but a cauterizing pain had begun to bore in behind her eyes, tightening her voice. She wanted nothing to do with tears. She needn't have worried; they didn't seem willing, finally, to come.

Randy was looking into a space of air just above the floor, but he raised his eyes and made himself look at her.

"I can't—easily say," he said at last. "It was something I had to do. Had to *have*. I was afraid—Alma," he said suddenly. "There was nothing you did. Nothing wrong with you. It was only me, I swear." His voice came breathy, in rushes.

"Nothing wrong with me," she repeated.

She thought a minute.

"Why did you not just leave? Long ago?"

He looked down again, rubbed his hands against the sides of his knees.

"To wait until Kira could handle it."

"So—when would that have been, if I hadn't—"

"Soon," he interrupted. "It would have been very soon."

In fact he hadn't known when he was going to tell her, or how he would undertake it. The thought always made his stomach wring. He would probably have waited until Darla forced him. It was the only time in his life he had not seized a task and run straight for the goalposts with it.

"I can't quite—how did you—Randy, did we not know each other?"

She asked in real bewilderment. It was the only thing left to ask: as if unable to place a stranger who had just hailed her heartily, full of anecdote. But her eyeballs ached dry in their sockets, and as the larger picture fanned open she felt suddenly reptilian, hideous, a toad-thing. Tended and tolerated in its plastic tray.

"Oh, Alma, please. Of course we knew each other. Of course we did. We had a good run. We had a good, long run. It's just that—things happen sometimes that don't—don't really have anything to *do* with—"

"I have no way of coming out of this," she said slowly.

THE GREAT FAR AWAY

Nothing was to be the same, and that was in many ways a relief. But the dawning comprehension that she was guilty, guilty by default, made her blink in wonder. Though he had obliterated the city of their marriage in a slow sandstorm—it was she who would be blamed. She would be seen as having failed, being insufficient to him. That was the first assumption. He'd had to seek for sufficiency elsewhere: therefore, her fault. An equation. Any court of human law would rule it. No division of responsibility chips. You were charged with the crime of your own loss. Loss and blame came at you from both ends of the same event, a two-headed snake.

I am Alma, insufficient to my husband. Crook. Loser.

Occupation? Faller.

Except, she thought, smiling sadly to herself: there is nobody there to catch me.

"Alma," Randy was saying. "Alma." A hypnotist, waking his subject. Bringing her to.

"Alma," he said. "Please don't make it harder. Please. I'll make sure you have everything you need. I'll talk with Kira in the morning."

The house breathed silently. She looked at him.

"You were someone I knew," Alma said.

The fourth and final event that took Ferris by storm was the marriage of Randy Winslow and Darla Messenger, the spring before their children took off for college in 1996. I have the letter here describing it—yes, the letter that set my reminiscence in motion, you see. Found it cleaning, remember—trying to throw out those useless papers; they seem to spawn themselves, do you notice? It came—the letter—from a woman whose identity I must protect, whose nature is kind, and you must take my word about that. Somewhere along the conveyor belt of her own disappointments—perhaps in combat against trendy cynicism, certainly to hold at bay the terrifying world outside Ferris—she adapted, some time back, a strict policy of positive thinking. Her belief—her need—for happy endings, was—is—very strong. I never answered her letter. Couldn't bring myself to. But I kept the thing. Don't know why, exactly, since it upset me so much.

Perhaps to remind myself of the story, whenever I'd next come across that infernal piece of paper.

It was a beautiful day. May weather just right, sunny and breezy. The whole tribe was invited. They held the ceremony in the Commons, and remember that new park area by the river? Rented especially from the town, for that day. A rock band played, and there was more sumptuous food than any of us had ever seen. Lobster, brie, steak, salmon, endless champagne, the best beers and wines. No expense spared. Everybody was there. People danced and ate and drank; it went on all day. Finally at twilight the cake was cut (towering! commissioned from good old Marlene!) and toasts were made—Rex made one, very jolly, and Caroline Everton made another, more sober and sincere, I'd say. Bram Parnell got up—he married Vera, you know—and presented Randy and Darla with a giant gouache portrait of the two of them, done from photographs he'd taken, framed under glass, with a big pink-and-blue satin ribbon tied around it. Ethan and Kira were standing around, watching the festivities together. When Darla badgered them they did dance one dance, but otherwise they wanted to hang back around the edges of the party. They seem the best of pals now, both of them startlingly beautiful—and very smart, very serious, you know. Ethan's been accepted at Brown and Kira at Amherst, can you believe it? Then Randy and Darla danced the spotlight slow dance. It was James Taylor's "Don't Let Me Be Lonely Tonight." Not a dry eye in the Commons, I promise. They've built a new house, did you know? Further up Patch Mountain—way above the suburbs—acres of woods all around; a huge oak deck and swimming pool, tennis court, in the house a film screening room and wine cellar. Their kitchen would pop your eyes out, and their bedroom has almost one entire wall of glass: they can see down over all of Ferris, all the streets and highways, practically out to Sequoia—Annie, you should see the lights across the land in that view, at night! Well, Randy looked kind of dazed, but happy of course, and Darla was dazzling. She seemed to radiate sunbeams.

These two have it made, and they look fantastic.

My friend did not mention in her letter where Graham or Alma might have been that day, that evening, or what they might have been doing. I'm sure she didn't know. Opportunities for such celebrations came so much more rarely by then, amidst the remaining tribe.

I have since learned other things from the letter writer. Kira completed her undergraduate work at Amherst, and afterward moved to a flat in a big, gingerbready Cambridge house with her boyfriend; they've enrolled in graduate school. Both of them plan to be structural engineers. Ethan took a bachelor's degree in philosophy, and, against his mother's protests, has since volunteered for the Peace Corps. He is working with villagers in Mali, West Africa, currently helping them assemble a pipe system for irrigation water.

Alma Collier stayed with friends in Lake Oswego, Oregon until the period when someone managed to alert her that Mavis Regan was in the final stages of breast cancer. That was in 1998. Alma flew back to Ferris to stay with Mavis, and cared for her to the last. Very few people glimpsed Alma during this time. Likely she and Mavis kept to themselves, and in truth there would have been but a handful of original tribe members in the area who might have recognized

Alma. By then Ferris was a spreading amoeba, a cumbersome "bedroom city," flanked by business parks and golf clubs and enormous, suburban tracts of identical, salmon-pink townhouses spaced about three feet apart—tracts reaching nearly to Sequoia, filled with harrassed, busy residents who commuted to work in gridlocked traffic, played tennis, chauffeured their kids, shopped at any number of malls and superstores, worked out, washed their cars. None of them would have any reason to know Alma Collier.

After Mavis Regan's death, Alma quietly departed Ferris for good. Rumors of what Alma had gone on to do—among those few individuals who tried to keep abreast of such things—ran a colorful spectrum; my friend the letter writer could not verify a one. In any case, Alma never appeared in Ferris again. Neither Congressman Winslow nor the elegant Mrs. Winslow, with her astonishing handshake, gave any indication in their dealings with the press or television media, or even to intimate colleagues and acquaintances, that the congressman had been married before. And if some did know about it, the congressman managed with such swiftness and charm to set these good people at their ease, warmly soliciting their own enthusiasms and habits, that they found themselves downright glad to be guided—so naturally, so comfortably—toward a more interesting question.

Not often, but once in a great while, a thought insinuates.
Is it possible I set the whole of it in motion?

If I had found a way to stay with poor Graham—if we had made our own baby—might things have wound their ways differently? Silly, but I can't help the thought from time to time. I imagine, for a fanciful instant, that had I acted differently it might have erased the chain, you see; the domino-fall. Sequence and consequence. But in the next breath, this little seizure begins to ebb away. If I'd stayed with Graham, perhaps things would have turned out worse. How can anyone presume to guess? You can't back up like a dump truck and unwill the actions of the past, much as we may long to. And you can never unwill children—though some people like to make such remarks when they're in great distress or trying to show off, or in some other desperate state. It doesn't matter, because children will always defy your secret will. And the children I am thinking of—they're fullblown adults now, staking out towns and families of their own.

Seeking their fortunes.

Sometimes I do wish that one of those children, all grown up, might one day find his or her way to me. From curiosity, or some sort of sixth-sense hunch. I could try then, maybe, to explain. To sketch a picture. In the next moment a prickle of heat flushes my face, angry with myself for entertaining such nonsense. As surely as breath follows breath, those young people have no earthly reason to care.

Now, I'm no music expert. But lately I've been listening, over and over, to a recording of Norwegian music I picked up in Paris, from an instrument that sounds like the ancestor of a Southern fiddle. In fact it is exactly that: the *hardingfele* or Hardanger fiddle, ancient Norwegian version. Named after a fjord, near the place where the oldest of these instruments was found. A beautiful thing it is. I've stared so long at the photo in the little booklet. Carved with designs of garlands of flowers and leaves like fossils, careful patterns around the sound holes. Inlaid with bone and mother-of-pearl. Pegbox, four or five strings. What I want to say is this: the instrument sings a queer, plaintive tune that circles back on itself, as if eternally. Patient and attending. Not asking that things be more or different than they are, but instead sort of chanting the mournful clearness of what is. And somehow the barren beauty of the fiddle's tune puts me at once in mind of the early years in Ferris: of wild, open pastures and oak-studded hills around worn wood houses. Of Patch Mountain, green in spring and gold in summer and fall; of the apple orchards and vineyards at its base, vibrant under the sun, of the salt smell and white ribbons of seafoam unfurling off Stone Cove and Moreno Bay. I can see again the movement of the people I knew as if I were above them looking down: a little band of souls like plucky shipwrecked Crusoes, scampering on the shore, sitting in groups on the sand at night, laughing and shouting at the stars. Behind them spreads the greenblue line of the far distance, patient and infinite, the uncharted place where speculation is made.